ARIZONA SHOWDOWN

Travis Jordan was a bounty hunter with his own reasons for turning his back on normal life. Then someone appeared from his past with a plea for help. Family duty reached for him, which he could not ignore, and he returned to his home range. But once he drew his pistol, he would be unable to holster it until the last shot in a bitter clean-up had been fired. It was kill-or-be-killed — and he was resolute that he would win . . .

Books by Corba Sunman
in the Linford Western Library:

RANGE WOLVES
LONE HAND
GUN TALK
TRIGGER LAW
GUNSMOKE JUSTICE
BIG TROUBLE
GUN PERIL
SHOWDOWN AT SINGING SPRINGS
TWISTED TRAIL
RAVEN'S FEUD
FACES IN THE DUST
MARSHAL LAW

CORBA SUNMAN

ARIZONA SHOWDOWN

Complete and Unabridged

LINFORD
Leicester

First published in Great Britain in 2006 by
Robert Hale Limited
London

First Linford Edition
published 2008
by arrangement with
Robert Hale Limited

Gloucestershire County Council	

823.9′2 [F]

ISBN 978–1–84782–054–9

Published by
F. A. Thorpe (Publishing)
Anstey, Leicestershire

Set by Words & Graphics Ltd.
Anstey, Leicestershire
Printed and bound in Great Britain by
T. J. International Ltd., Padstow, Cornwall

This book is printed on acid-free paper

1

Travis Jordan reined in on a bare ridge, his blue eyes narrowed against the dust cloud flaring from the wheels of the stagecoach surging along the trail below, his ears irritated by the insistent rumbling as the vehicle swayed and jolted across the rough terrain. He checked his surroundings for signs of Wink Carson's hold-up gang — if the outlaws did not strike soon they would lose the chance on this trip. The high Texas sun tortured the baked landscape, its rays almost too bright for human eyes, but Jordan saw no sign of furtive movement on the trail ahead and eased off the ridge to continue following the stage, remaining out of sight yet watching every yard of its progress to Amarillo.

For twelve years now, Jordan had followed the dangerous pursuit of bounty hunting, seeking out those desperadoes with a price on their heads and taking them dead or alive. He had discovered a natural facility for the grim work, and was respected by many lawmen over the whole south-west, his success a byword, his name a living legend that struck fear into the legion of outlaws plaguing the country.

His was a humourless life, driven as he was by the nightmarish memory of himself as a 12-year-old boy standing in the main street of Oak Bend, Arizona, gazing down at the blood-stained body of his mother lying dead from an outlaw's bullet — they had been caught up in a bank robbery gone wrong. From that day he had hated wrongdoers with every fibre of his powerful body, and had attuned himself to the grim life of manhunting, driven on by his own conscience, for he blamed himself for his mother's death, and his only satisfaction in life was putting an end to the evil men who preyed like wild animals on those living peacefully within the law.

The trail crossed a high plateau and then dipped down into a gorge with high walls that seemed to lean in to engulf the winding trail. Jordan pushed his gaunt buckskin in behind the coach, his eyes narrowed beneath his down-pulled Stetson as he looked for movement in the undisturbed heat haze that hung like a pall over the burnished rocks. The coach driver was working frantically with his reins, pressing his feet against the footboard and leaning backward to hold his team under control on the dangerous descent. The shotgun guard glanced back at Jordan and waved a hand in acknowledgement of his presence.

The guard faced his front again, and at that precise moment a shot crackled ominously, barely registering above the rumble and clatter of the big coach wheels. Dust was flying from the deep ruts of the trail and Jordan was hard put to peer through the choking screen that hung in the air behind the swaying vehicle, but he saw the guard half-rise

3

from his seat before pitching sideways off the coach. The man hit the ground hard and bounced lifelessly a couple of times before crumpling into an inert heap.

Jordan drew his pistol as the coach began to slow. He could hear the driver yelling at the team. He skirted the coach, reins gripped in his left hand, gun uplifted in his right, eyes narrowed for a first glimpse of the hold-up men. The coach stopped abruptly and dust began to settle. Jordan rode around the vehicle. Ahead, three riders were sitting their mounts across the trail, guns levelled at the driver, who slammed on his brake and dropped his reins to lift his hands shoulder high.

Wink Carson was holding a pistol in his right hand. Tall and heavily built, his fleshy face set in a ferocious scowl, Carson was easily recognized by Jordan, who had studied wanted posters of the gang before beginning his hunt for them. Carson's two accomplices were in the act of moving forward to grab the strongbox when Jordan appeared from the back of the coach.

'Hold it right there!' Jordan called. 'Drop your guns.'

He was not expecting the trio to surrender and, when Carson triggered his .45, Jordan fired instantly, his quick shot hitting the gang boss in the centre of his chest. The crash of the shooting blasted out the silence and raucous echoes fled down the gorge, greatly amplified by the closely retaining rock walls. Carson pitched out of his saddle and Jordan turned his deadly gun on the remaining two outlaws.

Both men were swinging to face him, their pistols turning black muzzles in his direction, and Jordan fired rapidly, his eyes narrowed against flaring gun smoke. His brain hardly registered the quick blast of the shooting. He drew a bead on the chest of the nearest outlaw, and was already shifting his aim as the man stiffened under the shock of striking lead. The remaining outlaw was having difficulty levelling at Jordan

— his stricken companion was between them — but Jordan fired a head shot that struck the man squarely between the eyes.

Echoes faded slowly, reverberating dully. The coach driver was motionless on his high seat, hands still raised, seamed face pale in shock. Jordan remained motionless for long moments, gazing at the three downed bandits while his mind savoured the slaughter. Then he reloaded the empty chambers of his pistol, returned the weapon to its holster, and stepped down from his saddle to begin the grisly task of checking the outlaws and tying them to their saddles.

'It is Wink Carson and two of his bunch.' The driver descended from the coach and stood over the fallen outlaws. 'Carson shot Billy — never gave him a chance to put his hands up.'

'Go take a look at him.' Jordan suggested. 'He might be alive; although I doubt it after the fall he took.'

The driver scrambled away around

the coach, his boots scraping obdurate rock. Jordan pushed back his Stetson and cuffed sweat from his wide forehead. His angular face was fixed in its habitual cold expression, unemotional, but a pulse of pleasure was beating somewhere in his mind.

A movement inside the coach attracted his attention and he turned swiftly as a woman's voice spoke to him.

'What is happening? Is it a robbery?'

Jordan found himself looking into the beautiful oval face of a young woman about eighteen years old. Her long hair was the colour of Kansan corn in August and she had pale blue eyes that were gazing questioningly at Jordan's face. A frown marred her smooth forehead. Her long blue travelling dress did not conceal the lines of her slender figure, and Jordan felt a pang of interest stab through the barren desert of his emotions. She was charming, completely different from the women he knew, and the unexpected sight of her toyed capriciously with his senses. He

7

realized that she was studying him intently and could probably see the quick interest in his narrowed eyes.

'It started out as a hold-up, ma'am,' he hastened to explain, 'but there's nothing to worry about now. It's all over and there's no danger to you. If you would sit down and relax, the coach will be on its way in a few moments.'

'There was shooting,' she insisted, her tone low and musical. 'Has anyone been hurt?'

Jordan glanced to the rear of the coach, where the driver's short, stocky figure was appearing, partially shrouded by still settling dust. The man shook his head, signifying that the guard was dead, and Jordan steeled himself against a rush of unaccustomed emotion that clutched at him despite his iron control, making him aware that the sight of the girl had penetrated his shield and enabled his captive soul to catch a glimpse of release.

'No one's hurting right now,' he

responded, 'but there are four dead men — three of them outlaws.'

She gasped audibly and shrank back into the coach. Jordan saw the swiftly changing expression on her face, and turned away to finish his grim chore of readying the outlaws for travel, his thoughts twisting in his mind. He was aware of the uselessness of pursuing bad men, for nothing could alleviate the pain in his heart, or bring back his mother.

'Billy's dead,' the driver said, shaking his head. 'Gimme a hand to put him inside the coach.'

'You'd better put the girl up on the seat with you,' Jordan suggested. 'She won't want to travel with a dead man.'

'You're right' The driver opened the door of the coach and encouraged the girl to alight.

Jordan gave his attention to readying the dead men for travel, and then helped the driver put the dead guard inside the coach.

'You shouldn't have any more trouble

on the run into Amarillo,' he said. 'I won't be able to keep up with you so you'd better get on. I'll see you when I hit town, huh?'

'Sure thing. And thanks for escorting us. What made you so certain Carson was gonna strike today?'

'I got the word,' Jordan replied, and stood watching while the driver regained his seat, picked up his reins, and set the team in motion. There was a crack of the whip, the grating of wheels, and dust flew as the coach resumed its journey.

Jordan tied the reins of the three horses together and led them in the wake of the coach. Amarillo lay four miles ahead, and he was content to take his time. He thought of the girl on the coach and experienced a trickle of emotion but stiffened himself mentally, for he was keenly aware that he could not relax his grim attitude and still work effectively.

Night was closing in when he sighted the outskirts of Amarillo. He rode along the main street and reined in outside the law office. Lights were showing in some of the windows along the wide thoroughfare, and he relished the sense of remoteness that gripped him as he dismounted.

Several men were standing in a small group on the sidewalk outside the office, and they crowded around the burdened horses, exclaiming at the sight of the dead men.

'Baldy Johnson told us Carson and his bunch held up the coach,' someone remarked. 'Did they put up much of a fight?'

'Nope. I surprised them,' Jordan replied tersely, and stepped on to the sidewalk.

He entered the office. Sheriff Taylor was seated at the desk, writing, and he looked up at Jordan's entrance; a big man well-set in middle-age, tall and fleshy, with dark, questioning eyes and a thin-lipped mouth. His hair was grey.

'Baldy said you were on your way in with Carson and two of his gang,'

Taylor said heavily. 'You did a good job, Jordan. Carson was getting to be a real nuisance. It'll take me a couple of days to get your money through, and I got a new dodger come in on one Bill Stoll, which I think will interest you.'

'Later,' Jordan replied. 'I need to get cleaned up, eat, and then sleep for a couple of days. Take care of those bodies out there, huh? They're all yours.'

'Sure. Let's take a look at them to establish their identities, and you better take heed I've had a report that Choya Vargas has been seen in town, asking questions about you. He's het up about the way you killed his two brothers and their crooked bunch last year.'

'There's always someone looking for me,' Jordan responded.

'I wouldn't have your job for anything,' the sheriff mused. 'Watch your back, huh?'

'I'll do that,' Jordan promised.

They left the office. The crowd outside had multiplied, and Taylor shouted for space around the horses. A silence fell while he examined the bodies in the yellow lamplight, lifting each dangling head in turn to scrutinize stiff features.

'Yep. You done a good job,' Taylor observed. He looked around at the intent faces of the townsmen. 'Joe, cut along to Ben Dix's place and tell him I got some business for him.'

A man hurried off into the shadows to fetch the undertaker. Jordan pulled his reins from the tie-rail and swung into his saddle.

'I'll be seeing you, Sheriff,' he said, and set off along the street to the livery barn.

He was bone-weary but his reflexes were sharp and he was aware of his surroundings as he rode along the darkened street, keeping to the centre of the broad thoroughfare, where the shadows were heaviest. He passed the Prairie Dog Saloon, its windows ablaze with yellow light, batwings swinging ceaselessly as men entered or emerged. The sound of a piano being pounded came from deep within the building, and Jordan moistened his lips at the thought of a tall glass of beer.

His hunger was deep-seated. Trail food had been his staple diet for more than a week, and now he was back in town his desires had quickened, but he staved them off. His horse came first, and he rode into the livery barn. He could still hear piano music in the distance as he stepped down from his saddle, but it was muted now, almost ghostly in the night, and he went through the routine of caring for his horse.

He carried his saddle-bags and Winchester when he left the stable, and walked back along the sidewalk to the saloon. His throat was parched and he needed a drink to cut through the trail dust that seemed to ingrain his innards. Thrusting through the batwings, he paused on the threshold to look around the big room, which was a hive of activity. About twenty men were present, some lining the bar and others sitting at gaming tables, intent upon the fall of the cards. The high volume of sound lessened for a few moments when he was first spotted, and all heads turned in his direction, for word of the fate of Wink Carson had filtered through the town after the arrival of the coach.

Jordan had two drinks and departed immediately. He was hungry, and walked through the shadows to Belle's Diner, which was crowded. Belle Martine, the owner, an ex-saloon girl turned entrepreneur, was seated with the town mayor, Frank Whitlock, who was eating supper, and she arose at the sight of Jordan and came towards him, smiling a welcome.

'Travis!' she exclaimed. 'I heard you were on your way in. How you been doing?' She glanced around the crowded room and held out a hand to him, sliding it under his elbow. 'We're extra busy tonight — I couldn't squeeze a starving gnat in anywhere. Come into the back room. It'll be more peaceful there.'

'Thanks, Belle,' Jordan replied. 'I'm

15

plumb starving. It's been a long week.'

Belle led him across the room. She was touching forty now, and her ample figure showed it. Her face was marred by extra flesh — small wrinkles around her generous mouth — and her blue eyes were surrounded by puffy skin and another patchwork of wrinkles. Her long blonde hair, piled up in an intricate French style, was laced with grey. She was the only person in town who treated Jordan as if he were a normal man.

'Gimme your order and I'll serve you myself,' she said, as Jordan sat down at a long table in the private room.

'I'm easy. I'll have anything that's going,' he replied, 'and plenty of it. I've been dreaming of this place for the last forty-eight hours.'

'You just sit there and relax and I'll soon have you eating,' Belle promised. 'I saw the stage pull in, and Baldy Johnson was full of what you did to the Carson bunch. You're sure making a big inroad into the crooked element around here. Sheriff Taylor reckons you're winning the battle against the bad guys, but you better watch out for Choya Vargas. That greaser has been seen around town the last couple of days. He's still sore that you killed his brothers last year.'

'Thanks for the tip, Belle.' Jordan dumped his saddle-bags on a corner of the table and leaned his rifle against the back of a chair. 'I've got a lot of unfinished business around, and it tends to catch up with me at odd moments.'

Belle nodded and departed into the kitchen, leaving the smell of cheap perfume in the air. Jordan heaved a sigh as he relaxed, stifling a yawn as tiredness nagged at his mind. He was between jobs now, and that was a situation he did not like. He drew his pistol and examined the cylinder, spinning it and testing the action, and then opened a saddle-bag, took out cleaning materials, and worked on the gun thoroughly while awaiting his meal.

Belle served him with a plateful of

hot food and sat with him, chatting about life around town while he ate. Generally, folk did not chat with Jordan. They were too aware of his violent way of life, and his appearance and manner did not foster a friendly atmosphere. People were afraid of him.

'Will you be around town long?' Belle asked when he had finished his meal and was rising from the table to leave.

'Hard to say,' he replied. 'Sheriff Taylor told me when I got in that he has a new paper on Bill Stoll, and I'll be riding out in the morning if I can get a lead on Stoll.'

'He's the killer who shot a sheriff in Waco, ain't he?' Belle asked.

'Yeah, and a youth was killed in the crossfire,' Jordan observed. 'Stoll needs killing. Thanks for the meal, Belle. It was the best I ever ate. See you around.' He flipped a dollar into her ready palm and departed.

The moment he reached the sidewalk he was aware that he had walked into trouble. A sixth sense triggered an alarm in his mind and he moved swiftly away from the restaurant's lighted window, lunging sideways into the dark alley beside Belle's Diner. A gun blasted across the street from him, belching reddish-orange flame, and a .45 slug hammered into the woodwork beside his head with a tearing thud.

Jordan dropped to the ground, palming his pistol as he did so. He cocked the weapon but did not return fire, and lay listening to the echoes fading across the town. When silence returned he prepared to move, but a voice spoke to him from the shadows at the corner of the alley.

'Jordan, I'm here to kill you,' the voice hissed through the shadows.

'Who are you?' Jordan demanded.

'Choya Vargas. You killed my brothers last year, and three of their men. We will fight.'

'Sure, if that's the way you want it. You want it fair or all in?'

'I'll stand up to you. Come on out into the light.'

'Not while you've got a gun across the street, waiting for me to show.'

Vargas shouted in Mexican, warning his pard to stay out of it.

Jordan remained on the ground for several moments, gun ready in his hand. He could see nothing of the Mexican, and heard nothing, but was aware that Vargas had not departed, and waited patiently for the Mexican's next move.

'I am armed only with a knife,' Vargas said suddenly. 'Will you use such a weapon, *señor*?'

'Sure.' Jordan got to his feet, holstered his gun and pulled a long knife from the scabbard at the back of his cartridge belt. 'It's your play,' he added.

The words were hardly out of his mouth when a shadow moved in the alley mouth. The blade of a knife glinted in reflected light. Jordan thrust up his saddle-bags and felt the jar of the knife striking hard. He swayed to his right and swung his knife, aiming for the

Mexican's left side. Vargas faded from the attack, and then came in again surprisingly swiftly, stabbing for Jordan's stomach. Jordan again used his saddle-bags to stop the blow.

Jordan could hear the heavy breathing of his opponent. Vargas was fast, and the shadows made him deceptive. The faint glint of naked steel swept in, missing Jordan's throat by a hair's breadth, and Jordan dropped to one knee, stabbing upwards, thrusting with all his strength. The point of his knife met resistance, overcame it, and slid up to the hilt into the Mexican's stomach.

Vargas uttered a shocked cry and blundered sideways, falling against the wall of the diner and losing his grip on his knife. The weapon clattered on the ground as he fell on his face. Jordan straightened, breathing heavily. He wiped his blade on the Mexican's jacket before sliding it back into its sheath, and then drew his pistol and bent over Vargas. The fingers of his left hand encountered the stickiness of

21

blood as he pressed the hand against the Mexican's chest. There was no heartbeat.

Holstering his gun, Jordan left the alley and went on his way, making for the hotel. Sheriff Taylor was standing in the doorway of his office, peering around in the darkness. He relaxed when he saw Jordan appearing out of the shadows.

'I guessed it was you involved with that shooting,' the lawman said.

'Vargas,' Jordan replied. 'He's dead in the alley this side of Belle's Diner. Figured to carve me up but I got lucky. I'm heading for the hotel now. I need to sleep.'

'I forgot to tell you when you came into town,' the sheriff said. 'There was a mighty nice gal got off the stage when it rolled in. The first thing she asked me was if I knew you, and she used your name. I said you'd be coming in with Carson and his two men, and she said to tell you she'll be waiting at the hotel to talk to you.'

Jordan frowned. He had not forgotten the girl on the coach.

'What could she want with me?' he demanded.

'I can't answer that,' Taylor said with a grin, 'but she can, and she's waiting at the hotel for you.'

Jordan went on, watching his surroundings. He pictured the girl in his mind, wondering about her. What had she been doing on the coach? Where had she come from and where was she going? Why had she asked for him by name? She evidently did not know him by sight for she had shown no sign of recognition at the scene of the hold-up, and he was certain he had never set eyes on her before.

The hotel lobby was busy. There were two men and a woman standing before the reception desk, and the girl he had seen on the coach was sitting on an easy chair set against the far wall. Jordan paused and studied her face, frowning as he searched his memory for a clue to her identity. She spotted him in the doorway and stiffened, her face showing a play of emotions as she gazed at him.

Jordan moistened his lips and crossed to where she was seated, holding her gaze. She got to her feet, smiling uncertainly as he approached.

'I'm Travis Jordan,' he said. 'The sheriff said you were asking after me when the coach pulled in. How come you don't know me by sight but know my name, and why do you want to talk to me?'

'Travis,' she replied. 'I recognize you now. My brother Lance looks a lot like you. I'm Hester Jordan, your sister.'

Jordan frowned as astonishment struck him. For a moment he was nonplussed and gazed at her searchingly, now able to see signs of their mother in her youthful face. She laughed nervously.

'I'm so glad I've found you,' she said softly, holding out a hand to him. 'It's been such a long time. I was only eight years old when you left Box J in Arizona.'

'That was a long time ago!' Jordan moistened his suddenly dry lips. 'Why are you here, Hester? Is there trouble at Box J?'

To his chagrin, Hester covered her face with her hands and burst into tears, and he gazed at her frowningly, suddenly at a loss for words or action.

2

Jordan gazed at Hester, his mind seething with unaccustomed emotion. He lifted a hand to her shoulder and the contact seemed to open a floodgate in her. Her slim shoulders shook with emotion as she sobbed. Jordan put an arm around her.

'I'm sorry!' she gasped, looking up at him, eyes shimmering with tears. 'It's the relief at finding you. I didn't think I would, Travis.' She produced a handkerchief and dabbed at her eyes. 'We've had bad trouble at the ranch. When Dad was shot, Lance went after the man who did it and was badly hurt.'

'Is Lance dead?' Jordan spoke stiffly, suddenly cold inside.

'No, but it was touch and go. He was shot in the chest, but Doc Merrill says he'll get over it. Our range is overrun with rustlers, and gunmen have taken over Oak Bend. Sheriff Holder can't do a thing about the situation, and I think he's given up trying. A man named Abel Farron moved on to the range about five years ago. He took over Dan McCarthy's place on Sweetwater Creek, and that's when the trouble started. Everyone says Farron is behind the rustling. He's got a tough outfit, and they're running wild around the county.'

Jordan's eyes glinted and he drew a long breath. 'And you came all the way from Arizona to find me,' he mused. 'You want me to go back with you, huh, and take care of the trouble, is that it?'

She nodded, her eyes refilling with tears as she looked at him.

'There's no one else I can turn to,' she said forlornly. 'It's a terrible situation, Travis. Can you do anything to help us?'

'Does Pa know you came for me?' he asked.

'No.' She shook her head emphatically. 'He was struck in the head by a

27

bullet, and although he has recovered from the wound he does nothing but sit around these days. He doesn't speak at all, and seems to be living in another world. I don't think he understands that Lance has been very ill.'

'Who's taking care of the place while you're away?'

'Jingle Bob is still the ranch foreman. He's holding the place together, but only because he hasn't raised his hand against the rustlers. They would have killed him if he'd stood up to them.'

'Good old Jingle Bob! So he's still alive and kicking.' Jordan shook his head as memory thrust up images of the past. He sighed, reaching a decision. 'OK, Hester, I'll take a look at the trouble. I'll ride out tomorrow for home range. You'll take the next coach west, huh?'

'Oh, Travis, I'm so relieved. It's been like a nightmare. I'll catch the next coach back to Arizona.'

'There's just one thing,' he said, and she looked keenly at him. 'I'll ride in as a stranger. No one on home range should be able to recognize me after this long time. I'll sift into the county and stay in the background while I look around and see what's doing. I'll find out who's causing the trouble, take care of them, and then ride out again. No one but you need ever know that I've been back. Will you agree to that?'

'Yes, if that's what you want, but it's wonderful to see you again after all these years and perhaps you'll reconsider when you've settled the trouble.'

'You've sure got a lot of faith in me,' he observed. 'But don't worry. If I can't handle your trouble then nobody can.'

'We've heard a lot of stories about you over the years,' she ventured.

'Don't believe half of them.' He patted her shoulder. 'Let's sit down in the bar and you can fill me in on what's been happening at home. I need to know the background to the trouble. It'll save me time when I get there.'

He escorted her into the hotel bar, seated her at a corner table, and then fetched drinks, unable to keep his eyes from her face because there was so much of their mother in her features.

'Abel Farron is the cause of all our trouble,' Hester said. 'He hadn't been on Sweetwater Creek more than a few days before he showed up at Box J, throwing his weight around. He claimed our boundaries adjoining his range were wrong and wanted many acres of our range, saying they rightfully belonged to him. There was a long legal wrangle over the dispute, and Farron was proved wrong, but ever since then he's been a thorn in our flesh. He's hired a really tough crew that terrorizes the whole county, and nobody dares stand up to them — those that tried were killed or forced to quit. Jim Coolidge was shot in the back and his C Bar went to Farron. Frank Billings stood his ground, lost all his cattle, and ended up bankrupt.'

Jordan nodded. An unscrupulous man had settled in a quiet community like a wolf amongst sheep, and there was only one way to root him out. He dropped his right hand to the butt of his pistol, filled with an insatiable fury that had been born in him at the awful moment when he had looked down upon his mother lying dead in the street, killed by an outlaw's bullet.

'You're a lot like your mother as I remember her,' he said softly.

'I know. I saw a tintype of her and it struck me that I've taken after her. I've often wondered why you left home, Travis, and never stayed in touch with your family. Was there trouble between you and Dad?'

'It was something like that,' he said. 'I'd rather not talk about it, Hester. It's still too painful to consider. Have you enough money for your fare home?'

'Yes.' She nodded. Her pale eyes were over-bright, threatening to shed more tears, but she smiled. 'I hope I've done the right thing, coming for you. With Dad out of his mind and Lance on the sick list, I had no one to turn to for help. I could only think of you.'

'You did the right thing,' he reassured

her. 'I'm family, and it's my duty to help.'

Jordan could not take his eyes off Hester's face, and when he saw something akin to fear show briefly in her expression he reached across the table and took hold of her hand.

'You've got nothing to be afraid of now,' he said.

'But I have,' she gasped. 'Curly Snape has just come into the bar.'

'Curly Snape?' he echoed.

'He's one of Abel Farron's top gun hands!' Hester's face had paled. 'What on earth is he doing here? I saw him in Oak Bend when I was getting on the coach, and he saw me. He must have followed me from Arizona. Oh, Travis, what shall we do?'

'You'll do nothing.' Jordan turned his head and glanced at the man standing in the bar doorway.

Curly Snape was tall and slim, with all the earmarks of a gunhand about him. He was wearing twin sixguns on crossed cartridge belts around his waist.

His Stetson was pushed back on his forehead to reveal a mass of black curly hair. His expressionless face had cold brown eyes, and he was looking at the patrons, hardly moving his head as his keen gaze took in the room.

'Stay here and I'll talk to him; find out what his business is,' Jordan said curtly.

Hester lifted a hand in silent protest. Jordan smiled as he got to his feet, but his eyes were filled with cold calculation as he walked to the door. His right hand was down at his side, the butt of his gun touching the inside of his wrist.

Snape looked at Jordan. He had not seen Hester yet, and now the girl was directly behind Jordan's big figure. Snape stepped sideways to his left to permit Jordan to pass but Jordan paused in front of him. Snape's eyes narrowed as he realized that he was being confronted.

'You're Curly Snape,' Jordan said.

'Sure. What's it to you?' Snape's gaze quickly judged Jordan, placing him in the category of being dangerous.

'What are you doing in Amarillo?' Jordan demanded. 'You ride for Abel Farron in Arizona.'

'How'd you know that?' Snape's dark eyes took on an unpleasant glitter. 'I get it,' he added. 'Hester Jordan must have come here to see you, and she's told you about me. Are you the guy she's planning to take back to Oak Bend to fight Farron?' He guffawed. 'From what I heard, you're gonna clean out the range of hardcases.'

Jordan smiled. 'So you followed Hester from Oak Bend, huh?'

'Just obeying my orders.' Snape shrugged his slim shoulders. 'Are you the man Hester wants for that job I mentioned?'

'And if I am?' Jordan countered.

'My job is to kill you quick. You ain't about to ride to Arizona and run wild on the range there.'

'I'll tell you something.' Jordan smiled. 'I don't think you're fast enough to stop me.'

Snape restrained his breathing. His teeth clicked together. He seemed to grow taller as he prepared for action, and then his right hand flashed to the butt of his holstered gun. Jordan matched the sudden movement. His pistol cleared leather before Snape could grasp his butt. Jordan's gun angled upwards, pointing its black muzzle in the direction of Snape's chest, and then exploded in smoke and flame. The crash of the shot blasted through the small room, rattling glasses and bottles on the bar.

Snape managed to clear leather, but Jordan's bullet had already bored through his chest, and his nerveless fingers lost their grip on his gun before it could cover Jordan. The weapon thudded on the floor and Snape's body followed it down. Jordan stepped back, and did not holster his gun. The bar was frozen in shock Men were gazing towards the prostrate figure on the floor, and a heavy silence descended as the echoes of the fatal shot died away.

Jordan exhaled sharply to rid his lungs of gun smoke. There was movement in the doorway and his gun lifted. A man peered around the door post, and then a pistol shoved its hard muzzle into view. Jordan fired instantly, his butt kicking hard against the heel of his hand. His bullet bored through the door post, and the man outside came forward into view with jerky steps, his gun hand falling away, his weapon dragging out of his lifeless grip.

Pacing forward, Jordan stepped over the second man and moved into the doorway to look around. The hotel lobby was deserted now, and Jordan could see two saddle-horses standing at the tie-rail outside. He turned back into the bar. Hester was on her feet, her face ashen, eyes wide in shock She came towards Jordan with a hand outstretched, and he placed his left hand under her elbow.

'Just take a look at the second man,' he suggested. 'Did he ride with Snape?'

Hester looked at the body in the

doorway and nodded.

'It's Al Bowman,' she said. 'Another of Farron's tough bunch.'

'So it's started already.' Jordan holstered his gun with a slick movement. 'There'll be two less when I start cleaning up on home range.'

'I half wish I hadn't come for you, Travis. It could end with you being killed.'

'Don't give it a second thought.' Jordan smiled.

Sheriff Taylor appeared in the doorway, gun in hand. He stared down at the two dead men and then looked enquiringly at Jordan.

'What happened?' he asked.

Jordan explained and Taylor holstered his gun. His gaze flickered over Hester's pale face and he nodded.

'So you'll be riding out for Arizona tomorrow, huh?'

'Hester will be going home on the next coach west. I'll head the same way in my own time.'

'And this was self-defence.' Taylor

pushed back his Stetson and wiped his sweating forehead. 'Maybe it is time you moved on, Jordan, if they're starting to come out of the woodwork at you. You've done a good job around these parts. I wish you all the luck on your home range.'

Jordan led Hester out of the bar and escorted her to her room.

'There's a westbound coach leaving in the morning at nine,' she told him. 'Couldn't you travel on it with me?'

'I'll need my horse when I get to Box J.'

'You could leave the horse here and pick it up later. We have a number of really good horses at the ranch. I don't want to lose sight of you now I've found you.'

He shook his head. 'Let's do it my way, Hester. I'll turn up at Box J in a couple of weeks. When you get home, just wait for me to arrive, huh?'

She nodded reluctantly, and Jordan left her, promising to see her off on the coach the next morning. He left the hotel and walked to the law office. Sheriff Taylor was looking through a pile of wanted dodgers, and smiled when he looked up and saw Jordan. He held out two posters, and Jordan glanced at them, his interest quickening, but then reminded himself that he was going home and placed the posters back on the desk.

'It's tempting,' he said. 'Especially Bill Stoll, but I've got a personal chore to handle before I can get back to work. I'll return, Sheriff, and then I'll carry on. I'm too deeply involved in hunting bad men to be able to give it up. I'll be obliged if you'll put the bounty money due to me in my bank account when it turns up.'

'Sure thing. You've earned that money, Jordan. I'll look forward to seeing you again in a few weeks, huh?'

Jordan took his leave. He stood on the sidewalk outside the law office and looked around, his thoughts remote, impersonal. As a man who lived without roots, his sense of loneliness was keen, despite the fact that Hester had turned up to shatter his way of life. He went along to the livery barn to check on his horse, and then bedded down in the hay loft, sleeping with his hand on the butt of his gun.

The sun was barely clear of the horizon when he awoke and prepared to ride out. He went to the diner for breakfast and then took his leave of Belle Martine.

'I'm taking a trip,' he told her, 'but I hope to be back in a few weeks.'

'Don't take any wooden nickels,' Belle warned.

Jordan went along to the hotel where Hester was sitting patiently in the lobby with a small case at her feet. He glanced at the clock on the wall behind the desk, and was relieved that the coach was due to arrive within thirty minutes and, when it arrived, the Butterfield Overland Stage was almost on time. Jordan carried Hester's case and saw her into a corner seat on the coach.

'Don't look out for me,' he warned,

as the driver climbed up to his high seat and took up his whip. 'I'll just show up, and then we'll get to work setting the range right. Don't worry about anything, Hester.'

The driver cracked his whip and Jordan stepped away from the coach. The six-horse hitch threw their weight into their collars and the coach took off in a pall of dust that flew up from the wheels. Jordan watched the vehicle swaying and jolting until it was out of sight, and then sighed and went to the stable to fetch his horse.

He stopped off at the general store to replenish his supplies and, minutes later, rode out of town, turned his face to the west, and started the long ride back to home range. The prospect of the trip across New Mexico and into Arizona did not daunt him. He was accustomed to spending days at a time in the saddle, and did not mind the loneliness of the open trail . . .

Time passed monotonously, the days marked by an endless round of nightfall and dawn, the nights cold and cheerless and the daylight hours filled with the rigours of riding south-west. He crossed the Texas/New Mexico line and continued, his horse loping and trotting by turns, traversing a rolling land of rock and grassy plain, sometimes semi-desert and, in the far distance, the outlines of pale bluffs showed but seemed to draw no nearer.

He found a cattle trail that headed for Santa Fe and followed it part of the way, enjoying the easier going, his horse running effortlessly over grass or ploughing hock-deep through sand, but always travelling towards the setting sun. After endless days he finally reached Arizona range, and continued steadily, aware that he was now closer to home than he had been in many years. For a time he rode in the direction of distant Tucson before veering away west and north towards home range.

The nature of the country had changed imperceptibly to one of valleys of purple sage, low foothills, and a profusion of meandering streams and grey cedar flats that stretched to the south where buttes and canyons barred the way. Still Jordan rode on, now beginning to recognize landmarks. He crossed a sage flat, rode through a belt of timber and entered a canyon which he followed until it opened out upon undulating rangeland. Then suddenly, in the middle-distance he spotted the huddle of buildings that was Oak Bend, nestling on the bank of a narrow stream.

For a long time Jordan sat his horse and gazed at the town where his mother had been killed in the main street, while hurtful memories boiled up in his mind. His face looked as if it had been carved from granite, and such were the images passing through his mind he was oblivious to everything but the painful past.

When he went on he avoided Oak Bend, circling to the north-west until he struck the trail that would take him into the yard of Box J. He looked around at familiar sights, faintly surprised that everything was as he had seen it last — years before. Nothing seemed to have changed, and he rode the last miles home with his heart overburdened by ghosts of the past.

When he caught the faint echoes of a distant rifle shot he was instantly alerted. The sound came from the direction into which he was riding, and he galloped up a rise and reined in on the skyline, his keen gaze sweeping across the broad range. Movement caught his attention and he spotted a rider coming fast towards him, bent low in his saddle to get the last ounce of speed from his labouring mount. Two riders were moving in deadly pursuit some fifty yards in the rear and, even as he sighted the trio, gun smoke puffed from the pursuers and the crash of shots reached Jordan's ears.

He reached for his field glasses focusing quickly on the leading rider, and his teeth clicked together when he recognized the lean features of Jingle Bob Jones, his father's foreman. Jones was having trouble staying in his jolting saddle, and blood was showing on his left shoulder.

Jordan suspended his glasses from the saddlehorn and drew his saddle gun. Jones was coming along the trail that led to Oak Bend and was riding directly to the spot where Jordan sat his horse. The two pursuing riders fired again at Jones, and Jordan lifted his rifle to his shoulder, scared that Jones would be shot again before he could intervene. He jacked a shell into the chamber of his rifle and narrowed his attention to the foremost of the pursuers.

The crack of his Winchester threw a string of echoes across the range and the .44.40 slug struck the horse of the nearest pursuer. The animal's front legs buckled and it went down in a cart-wheeling fall that made Jordan grimace. The rider pitched headlong from his saddle and thumped heavily on the hard trail. Jordan reloaded and turned his attention to the second man, who was reining about and turning to flee. Jordan's rifle hammered again and the rider took the slug between his shoulder blades. He fell forward over the neck of his horse and then slid out of the saddle to lie inertly on the ground.

Jones came on as if nothing had happened. He saw Jordan sitting his horse on the ridge, had thrown a glance over his shoulder to see his pursuers down, and was wondering who had come to his aid on a range where he knew every man's hand was against him.

Jordan stepped down from his horse and grasped the reins of Jones's horse as the ranch foreman reined in. When the animal stopped, Jones slid sideways out of leather. Jordan caught and lowered him to the lush grass. Jones was only semi-conscious, his eyes half-closed and his eyelids flickering. Jordan fetched the canteen from his horse, uncorked it, and gave the foreman a drink, then poured a liberal amount of water over the man's left shoulder.

'Travis, is that you?' Jones demanded, breathing heavily. He opened his eyes fully and gazed up at his saviour. 'It is you,' he said. 'I thought I was dreaming.'

'Did Hester tell you I was coming?' Jordan demanded.

'Hell no! I told her to fetch you, and she needed some persuasion. When she showed up again a few days ago she admitted that she'd seen you in Amarillo but wouldn't say if you were coming or not. But here you are, and you couldn't have turned up at a better time. I was in a tight spot back there. They would have killed me for sure if you hadn't horned in.'

Jordan inspected Jones's shoulder while the man was talking.

'You'll have to go into town and get this looked at by the doctor, Jingle Bob,' he said. 'The bullet went clear through without touching bone, so

47

you've had some luck. Who were the two killers chasing you?'

'A pair of Farron's best gunnies. They meant to put me under.'

'Let's get on to town and get you checked out by the doctor. Can you ride?'

'I want to go back to Box J,' Jones said firmly. 'There was trouble back there when I left. You better ride on ahead of me, Travis. There's no telling what is going on at the spread. Most of the outfit up and quit yesterday, and there are only a couple of men with Hester, Lance and your pa.'

'OK, come back to the spread at your own pace.' Jordan jumped up and went to his horse. He swung into the saddle and hit the trail at a run, heading fast for Box J, familiar with every yard of the range, and counted off the distance as he pushed his horse to its limit.

He heard the sound of shooting while he was still some distance out from the spread, and rode to a vantage

48

point to take stock of the situation. The scene that awaited his eyes when he breasted a rise had him reaching for his Winchester, and was worse than anything he could have imagined.

3

The neatly laid-out Box J ranch was partially obscured, for the cook shack was burning furiously and a drifting column of smoke stretched up into the wide blue sky. From his elevated position, Jordan counted six spots around the yard from which shots were being fired at the house. He saw two rifles returning fire from the front of the building and one weapon firing from the rear at another attacker trying to sneak in from that direction. He lifted his Winchester from its boot and worked the lever. Dismounting, he dropped into cover and began to fire at the men shooting into the front of the house.

His first shots changed the situation. Echoes rumbled across the wide space as he selected targets and squeezed the trigger. The man nearest his position suddenly flopped down on his face and lay still. A second man twisted and relaxed. The third man jumped and spun around before he died, and the fourth hunched over his rifle and took no further part in the action.

But Jordan's intervention was noted, and the two remaining attackers directed fire at his position, splattering it with questing lead. He stayed low and traded shots with the attackers, but they decided to call off the raid and ran for their horses. Jordan chivvied them with shots as they mounted up and rode out, wounding at least one of them.

He stopped shooting when they were out of range, and stood and reloaded his Winchester while taking stock of the situation. The assailant at the rear of the house had also departed quickly. Jordan had hit four men in the brief fight, and did not expect the survivors to return until they had fetched reinforcements. He returned his rifle to its boot, mounted his horse and rode down into the ranch.

Hester appeared on the porch as Jordan crossed to the house. She was holding a rifle. Her left cheek was smeared with dust. Two cowboys emerged from the house and stood beside her, both holding rifles, and a young man appeared in the doorway. His right shoulder and chest were swathed in bandages, his right arm fastened in a sling. He was holding a pistol in his left hand.

'Travis!' Hester propped her rifle against a post, ran to Jordan as he dismounted, and threw herself into his arms. 'I was praying for you to show up. I knew you would be arriving any day now, but this was the time we needed you most. I never saw shooting like yours. How many of those sidewinders did you hit?'

'I would have got them all if they hadn't split the breeze,' Jordan said briefly. 'Two more minutes would have seen it through. I ran into Jingle Bob on the trail, being chased by two gunnies. He's got a bullet hole through his left shoulder, and said the ranch was under attack. You didn't exaggerate when you told me in Amarillo that you have trouble here. What was going on? Did that bunch just ride in and start shooting?'

'Two of Farron's men showed up first, demanding money — Fletch Braska and Hack Ritson. They boss all Abel Farron's dirty work. They said Pa owed Farron money, and if we couldn't pay cash they'd take stock in lieu. I don't know why they bothered because they've just about cleaned out the range. We'll be lucky if there are more than a few hundred head of cattle left out there. When I refused to acknowledge the debt, they threatened to send in a bunch of hardcases and ride roughshod over us. I thought they were bluffing, but, a couple of hours after they left, a bunch of gunnies showed up and tried to swarm all over us.'

'I know the name Fletch Braska,' Jordan mused. 'He's a two-bit gunman whose real name is Fletcher Sherwin.

He calls himself Braska because he hails from Nebraska. I've seen a dodger on him. He's wanted for bank robbery and murder. So this is where he's hiding out, and still causing trouble for honest folk. I'll look him up when I can get around to it.'

While he was talking, Jordan was watching the young man standing in the doorway, and could tell that he was gazing at his younger brother Lance — the family resemblance was uncanny. Hester noticed the direction of his gaze and addressed the two watching cowboys.

'Charlie, Tom, see if you can do something about the cook-shack, will you?'

The punchers nodded and hurried off across the yard. Hester grasped Jordan's arm and led him across the porch.

'Travis, this is your brother Lance,' she introduced.

'Howdy, Lance,' Jordan greeted. 'How you doing? Hester told me you'd been shot.'

'Glad to see you, Travis.' Lance grinned and nodded, his blue eyes gleaming. 'I been hearing a lot of the tales they tell about you, brother, and I took most of them with a pinch of salt, but what you did to that thieving bunch of rustlers makes me think you're twice the man they say you are.'

'It looks like I got a lot of work to do around here,' Jordan mused. 'So tell me about the set-up. I got it that Abel Farron is in the big saddle. How many riders has he got on his payroll?'

More than twenty or he had that number before you showed up, but he's not in his crooked business alone.' Lance's eyes were bitter as he gazed out across the yard. 'I heard tell that Two-Finger Dack, who owns Flying D, and Pete Hillyard of Circle H, are in with Farron. Rustling is big-time around here, and everybody who is anybody is cutting himself a slice of the action. The law is worse than useless, Travis. Sheriff Holder is a sheriff in name only, and sticks around town all the time. Nobody else will take the job.'

'It sure looks like I've picked myself a big chore,' Jordan mused.

'You can't fight all the rustlers in a stand-up fight, Travis,' Hester said. 'They'd trample you underfoot. It would take an army to beat them. It would help if you could call on Sheriff Holder for assistance, but he's a big joke around here, and that's why the rustlers let him remain in office, although they put one of their men, Frank Lyle, into Holder's office as a deputy to keep an eye on the sheriff.'

'What about your neighbours?' Jordan asked. 'You must have some friends among them.'

'There's too much opposition for them to want to take a hand.' Hester shook her head. 'We're on our own, Travis.'

'Well, I'm here now.' Jordan looked around. 'You two stay close to the house and watch out for more trouble. I'll check over the place, and take a look at those men I shot. If you see any movement out there just fire a warning shot, huh?'

Hester nodded and Jordan went across the yard to the cook-shack. The two cowboys were watching the fire burning, helpless to save the building.

'Forget it,' Jordan told them. 'We can build another shack. Let's take a look at the men I shot. What are your names?'

'I'm Charlie Pierce,' said one. He was tall and thin, in his early twenties, dark-eyed and determined.

'Tom Baldwin,' said the other, a grin spreading across his fleshy face. He was short and wide-shouldered. 'I got to say I ain't seen shooting like yours. It was great.'

'Comes from long practice,' Jordan observed. 'How come you two stayed on when the outfit quit?'

'We got nowhere else to go.' Pierce shrugged. 'Although I don't reckon we can last much longer, the way Farron will hit us when he hears what you did to his men.'

'I killed two of his men who were

chasing Jingle Bob,' Jordan said. 'I guess we'd better work out some kind of a plan. It wouldn't do to be caught flat-footed the next time the hardcases come at us. I wanta ride into town and check on the law situation. It can't be as bad as Hester says.'

'It is.' Baldwin shook his head. 'The minute you show your face in Oak Bend, Frank Lyle will be at you. He don't take kindly to strangers showing up.'

'That's Farron's deputy, huh? Well, I plan to look him up soon as I can.'

They walked around the yard checking on the men Jordan had shot and found three dead and the fourth at his last gasp. Two of the men's horses were standing by the corral, and Jordan saw the Rafter F brand on them.

'Get a team hitched to the buckboard and load these bodies in it,' Jordan directed. 'One of you can drive it into Oak Bend. I'm expecting Jingle Bob to show up any time now, and he'll need a lift into town to see the doctor.'

He walked back to the house and, as

he reached the porch, Hester called out to him.

'Jingle Bob is coming in now,' she reported.

Jordan turned to see the wounded ramrod riding in through the gateway, slumped in his saddle and hanging on to his saddlehorn. The horse came across the yard and Jordan stepped down to grasp its reins as it halted. Jingle Bob slid out of leather and sprawled on the ground.

'What happened here?' he demanded, trying to rise.

'There were seven hardcases shooting at the house when I showed up,' Jordan told him. 'I killed four of them and the rest rode off. We'll stop your wound bleeding and then take you into town in the buckboard, Jingle Bob. Just stay quiet and we'll get things under way. I don't want the family here the next time Farron's bunch shows up.'

The ramrod slumped and gave up trying to stand. His face was ashen, his eyes filled with anguish. Hester hurried into the house to fetch bandaging.

'We need an outfit badly,' Jingle Bob said through his teeth.

'Why did your crew quit?' Jordan asked. 'Cowpunchers usually fight for their brand.'

'The odds were too great for them. They knew there could be only one ending in a fight like this, and nobody wants to die young. I don't blame them for quitting.' He grinned crookedly. 'There've been a couple of times when I felt like pulling my stakes. But now you're here we'll get 'em by the tail with a downward pull. Farron and his crooked sidekicks will wish they left Box J alone.'

'You said it, pard.' Jordan smiled. 'Stay quiet until Hester has bound you up. We're all going into town, and I'm leaving my family there while I handle Farron.'

'You'll be a better man than I already think you are if you can get Hester to quit this place,' Jingle Bob said, and lost consciousness.

Jordan straightened and looked around. Lance was motionless on the porch, and Saul Jordan had appeared and was standing beside his youngest son. Travis gazed at his father, shocked by his appearance. Saul was in his mid-fifties, but looked ten years older. His hair was predominately grey. Deep lines etched his mouth. His shoulders were stooped, and his left arm twitched spasmodically, his fingers trembling continually.

'Dad!' Jordan went forward, his eyes narrowed. He held out his hand as emotion flared in his mind.

Saul looked at the outstretched hand and then gazed into Jordan's face, his blue eyes expressionless. He gave no sign of recognition, and Jordan let his hand fall to his side. Saul turned and shambled back into the house, stumbling and colliding with the half-open door in passing. Jordan started forward but Lance grasped his arm.

'Don't bother, Travis. You can't do anything for him. He's been like this since he was shot. He doesn't know anybody and hasn't spoken a word. Doc says he might wake up one morning and be back to normal, and that thought has kept us going, but it doesn't seem likely that he'll recover.'

'Who shot him? Where did the shooting happen?'

'He was on his way into Oak Bend to pay eight thousand dollars into the bank — money from the sale of some cattle — but he never reached town. He was found lying in White Oak gully, his money missing. The ambusher's bullet struck his head a glancing blow, and left him as you see him now.'

'When did it happen?' Jordan asked.

'A little more than two months ago.' Lance was looking around the approaches to the yard, and suddenly raised his pistol and pointed in the direction of the distant town. 'A couple of riders coming in,' he warned.

Jordan turned and saw the riders, who were jogging leisurely towards the ranch.

'Who are they?' he demanded.

'Braska and Hack Ritson.' Lance sounded worried. 'They're the best of Farron's bunch. I've heard that Braska runs the rustling for Farron.'

'Good.' Jordan nodded. 'There's nothing like starting with the cream of the opposition. If I beat these two then the rest will be easy. You stay out of it, Lance. I don't want you mixed up in any shooting.'

'Don't sell them short, Travis. Braska is hell on wheels, and Ritson ain't no slouch I saw them in action in Oak Bend once, when they gunned down Pete Anders for standing up to them, and never forgot it. I don't reckon there's anyone faster.'

'There's always someone faster,' Jordan said softly.

Hester emerged from the house, carrying cloths and a bowl of water. She paused on the porch and looked at the approaching riders.

'Who's coming?' she asked.

'Braska and Ritson,' Lance told her.

'They were here earlier,' Hester

observed. She set down the bowl of water. 'I'd better get my rifle.'

'You and Lance better stay in the house until I've seen them off,' Jordan suggested.

'Not on your life,' Lance retorted. 'I wouldn't miss this for anything. If you're gonna shoot it out with them then I want in.' He checked his pistol and blew dust off the cylinder.

The riders turned in at the gate and came across the yard, their horse's hoofs raising tiny puffs of dust from the arid ground and rattling on the hard surface. Jordan watched them closely, recognizing Braska immediately from the wanted dodger he had seen. The outlaw was tall in the saddle, wide-shouldered and powerful. His bold features were coarse, wolfish, with merciless brown eyes glinting under heavy brows. He wore two guns on crossed cartridge belts, and his right hand did not stray far from his butt. Ritson was a much older man with a leathery face and sneaky eyes. His holstered pistol was on his left hip, butt forward.

Jordan stood on the edge of the porch, his back to the house, gun hand down at his side, waiting patiently for the pair to arrive. Hester picked up the bowl and left the porch to go to Jingle Bob's side. She knelt in the dust and busied herself with caring for the wounded foreman.

Braska and Ritson reined up six feet from the porch, and both hardcases gazed at Jordan.

'Who are you?' Braska demanded. 'I ain't seen you around before.'

'That's your good luck,' Jordan replied. 'But your luck has changed now I'm here, and I can sure recognize you, Braska. I've seen your face on a wanted dodger back in Texas. What are you doing riding for a crook like Farron? Did the law get too hot for you? How come you've quit robbing banks?'

Braska's expression did not change but his eyes glinted, and the fingers of his right hand twitched convulsively before lifting to hover above the butt of his gun.

'Are you a lawman?' Ritson spoke as if the words burned his mouth, spitting them out in a low, harsh voice.

'I never wore a law badge in my life,' Jordan asserted. 'What's your business? If you've come to check up on the riders you sent helling in here then you'll find four of them stretched out ready for burial. I guess you've overplayed your hand this time.'

'Who are you?' Braska demanded. 'I like to know a man's name before I kill him.'

'Names don't matter a damn.' Jordan smiled. 'I'm here to stand up against Farron, and anyone who rides in to make trouble. What's on your mind, Braska? Spit it out before the shooting starts.'

'We found two of our men dead on the trail between here and town,' Ritson said. 'Did you shoot them?'

'I had that pleasure.' Jordan nodded.

'I've declared open season on the Farron outfit, and I've made a good start today. Now it's your turn to face the music. Either of you can open the play. All you got to do is make a move toward your guns and I'll start shooting.'

A deadly silence followed. Braska and Ritson were shocked by Jordan's confidence and his brazen challenge. Braska did not move a muscle, but Ritson's hand eased toward his gun, fingers splaying slightly before he grasped his butt and pulled the weapon fast.

Jordan's pistol leaped into his hand and blasted off a shot that smacked out the silence with raucous intensity. The bullet smashed Ritson's sternum, bored through his heart and lodged itself in his left armpit. The gunman reared up in his saddle under the impact, his gun, half-drawn, falling from his suddenly nerveless fingers. He slumped sideways, falling against Braska, who fended him off with a powerful arm. Ritson plunged out of his saddle. His horse cavorted nervously, snorting in fear, and then swung and galloped off across the yard. Ritson's left boot caught in a stirrup and he was dragged away, spilling his blood into the receptive dust.

The echoes of the shot faded quickly. Jordan was motionless, his muzzle pointing at Braska, who did not move and looked as if he were frozen in disbelief. He was shocked by Jordan's gun speed. His hands moved slowly away from his waist, palms forward, and his face was stricken.

'Looks like you've changed your mind about causing trouble here,' Jordan said. 'What did you come for?'

Braska did not reply. He sat motionless, staring at Jordan, who holstered his pistol with a deft movement.

'It's your turn now, Braska,' Jordan resumed. 'Start the play any time you feel ready.'

'I ain't drawing against you.' Braska shook his head emphatically.

'Then disarm yourself, and do it

slowly — finger and thumb only, one gun at a time.' Jordan palmed his gun and cocked it, aiming its black muzzle at the centre of Braska's chest.

Braska divested himself of his twin Colts, letting them fall into the dust. He looked as if he were in a trance, unable to take his eyes off the deadly pistol in Jordan's hand.

'If you've got a hideout gun then get rid of it now,' Jordan continued.

Braska reached into his left armpit and brought a short barrelled .38 pistol into view which he tossed into the dust.

'Now get down off that horse.' Jordan waggled his pistol, and the outlaw dismounted quickly and stood with his hands raised. 'So you're Farron's top gun, huh? Well, you don't look so hot to me. If you're the best Farron can do then he's on the trail to hell right now.'

'You can't fight Farron's bunch,' Braska blustered. 'He's got an army he can send in here. They'll trample you into the dust, no matter how good you are.'

'Do tell!' Jordan smiled and motioned with his pistol. 'Give those two cowboys a hand with loading your dead hard-cases in the buckboard. We're going into town, and you're heading for jail. It'll be a long time before you taste freedom again. I seem to recall that you're wanted for murder as well as robbing banks.'

Braska obeyed sullenly and Jordan stood watching him until the buckboard had been loaded with its grisly freight. Then Braska was hogtied and put into the wagon, and Jingle Bob was lifted carefully and laid on straw at the back. Hester sat beside the wounded ramrod and Lance fetched his father out of the house and they climbed into the buckboard. Hack Ritson's horse had stopped at the gate, and stood with the dead killer's boot still trapped in a stirrup.

'I'm not staying in town,' Hester said, as Charlie Pierce tied his horse at the rear of the wagon and then climbed into the driving seat. 'If we leave the spread deserted, Farron will send men to either burn it or take over.'

'Don't worry yourself about Farron,' Jordan declared. 'You'll be safer in town so that's where you'll stay. I shall be able to do what I have to much better with the family out of my way.'

'How are you going to fight the rustlers?' Lance demanded.

'I haven't worked that out yet.' Jordan smiled grimly. 'I have an idea though.' He reached a sudden decision. 'In fact, I'm not going to ride into town with you. I can be more use by approaching this trouble from another angle, but I'll want you to do exactly what I say. Stay in town when you get there. Tell the sheriff that Braska is a wanted killer. I'll drop into town later and tell him about it.'

'What are you going to do?' Hester demanded.

'First, I'm gonna run a bluff on Farron.' Jordan smiled. 'If it works then Farron will be on his way out of this crooked business.'

'And if it fails?' Hester persisted.

'That hardly bears thinking about.' Jordan's voice was suddenly edged with tension. 'Off you go, and leave me to do what I came home for.'

Hester nodded slowly, and the buckboard lurched forward and started for the distant town. Jordan watched for some moments, nodding his approval when Tom Baldwin paused at the gate and boosted the dead Ritson across his saddle and led the animal behind the buckboard. Jordan looked around the Box J yard, his face hardening in expression when he regarded the burning cook-shack, and then swung into his saddle and rode off to the north. He wanted to take advantage of surprise, and headed for Farron's spread, ready to push the fight he had taken on for the sake of his family.

4

The Rafter F ranch sprawled along a creek that was fed by water draining from the Coulee Mountains in the north. The house was two-storey, large and four-square, with leafy trees planted around it for shade. A tall barn was to the left of the house, standing almost on the bank of the creek. There were two corrals, a bunkhouse, cook-shack and several minor buildings scattered around the hard-packed yard. A wrangler was busting a horse in one of the corrals — dust rising as the spirited animal bucked and sun-fished under the raking spurs of its tormentor, whose job it was to break its spirit. Several men were standing around the corral, watching the struggle for supremacy between man and beast.

Jordan reined in on high ground and studied the ranch. Before he had left for

73

other parts this spread had belonged to Colonel Dan McCarthy, and there had been no trouble on the range. Now Abel Farron was in the big saddle, and rustling was rife across the county. Reining forward, Jordan was impatient to get his first look at the man reputed to be the cause of all the local trouble. He followed the trail to the yard, where he was confronted at the gate by a rider toting a rifle across his saddlehorn.

'What's your business?' The guard was hard-eyed, expressionless, and the muzzle of his rifle gaped at Jordan's chest.

'I'm looking for a job. I was told to ask for Abel Farron.'

'You'll find him at the house.' The guard motioned with his rifle. 'But he ain't taking on new hands now.'

Jordan nodded and rode through the gateway. He crossed the yard, his keen eyes missing nothing of the scene around him, and dismounted in front of the porch. As he wrapped his reins around a tie-rail a big, powerfully built man emerged from the house and paused to look at him, planting his big feet on the creaking boards of the porch and putting his hands on his hips. The newcomer was dressed in dark range clothes and wore a wide-brimmed black Stetson. A cartridge belt encircled his thick waist and his right hand slid down to rest by the protruding butt of the pistol on his right hip.

'Who in hell are you and whaddya want?' he demanded roughly.

'I'm looking for Abel Farron,' Jordan replied.

'And what do you want with him?'

'I was told to ask for him — about a job.'

'We ain't hiring right now, so get outa here.'

'Are you Farron?' Jordan could read the obvious signs on the man. Here was a gunhand first and foremost, and probably the ranch foreman to boot; a man without conscience who relied on a gun to solve all his problems. His hard eyes carried no hint of gentleness, and his stance showed an eagerness for aggression.

'My handle is Sam Tate,' he rasped. 'I run this spread, and I'm telling you we don't need any extra hands right now. So split the breeze, mister.'

'I came here to speak to Farron, and I ain't leavin' until I've done so.'

'Is that so?' Tate leered and came down off the porch. 'If you ain't careful how you talk you won't get the chance to leave at all. Three men are buried down by the creek. They rode in asking for work, and couldn't take 'no' for an answer. I planted two of them myself and the boss nailed the third. We don't like strangers riding in here, so get the hell out pronto.'

'I was told I'd get a job here if I rode in,' Jordan persisted.

'What sonofabitch told you that?' Tate was becoming agitated. His eyes narrowed, filled with lust, and he worked the fingers of his right hand as it crept closer to his gun.

'I came through Oak Bend this

morning and saw Frank Lyle,' Jordan bluffed. 'Frank and me go back a long ways, and he told me to ride in here, so I wanta talk to Farron.'

'Any friend of Frank Lyle is a friend of mine,' a voice cut in from the doorway of the house.

Jordan shifted his gaze to the small, narrow-shouldered man who had appeared. The newcomer was dressed in a smart blue store-suit and highly polished shoes. His jacket was unbuttoned, revealing a spotless white shirt. A black string tie around his neck seemed too tight. His head was rather large for his small body. His features were small, eyes tiny but bright like a weasel's. He was hatless, and the top of his head was bald — what hair he had around the sides was short and iron grey.

'Abel Farron?' Jordan enquired.

'That's me. I heard what you said about knowing Lyle, and if he sent you here then I'll be happy to give you a job. What else did Lyle tell you?'

'He said you're running the rustling.'

'If he told you that then he must trust you completely. Anyone else running off at the mouth like that would collect a slug pretty damn quick.'

'Now see here, Abel, we got too many on the payroll as it is,' Tate protested harshly. 'You said we don't need more gunhands. The word is getting out what we're doing, and pretty soon we'll have the law riding in asking questions.'

'I own the law in these parts.' Farron's dark eyes glittered. 'Go get my buggy ready like I told you, Sam. I need to go into town today, not tomorrow. Take care of the chores around here and leave me to handle the business as I see fit.'

'I don't like the look of this guy.' Tate's mind was on a one-track trail. He glowered at Jordan. 'I smell trouble on him.'

'Do you know him from someplace?' Farron pushed aside the lapel of his jacket to reveal a shoulder holster in his left armpit.

'Never set eyes on him before.' Tate

shook his head. 'But there's something about him that grates in the mind, and I've never been wrong yet about a man. Take him on and you'll be sorry.'

'What's bugging you, Sam? I never heard you talk this way before. Are you losing your nerve?'

'You know better than that, so don't paint me yellow.'

'You're beginning to talk like an old woman who's been eating chicken-feed! Get outa here and make ready to ride into town with me. I'll handle this.' Farron's cold eyes studied Jordan. 'What name do you go by?'

'You pick one for me,' Jordan replied. 'I've forgotten the one my mother gave me.'

'What was your father's name?' Tate remained where he was despite Farron's orders.

'I never asked him.' Jordan smiled. 'Move your hand any closer to your gun and I'll tag you as unfriendly. If you've a mind for gun play then turn your hand loose and I'll go along with you.'

The raw challenge in Jordan's tone made Tate's pale eyes glitter. The fingers of his gun hand curled and he exhaled deeply. For a moment, Jordan thought the big ramrod was going to rise to his bait.

'Knock it off, Sam,' Farron said urgently. 'I take your point about not trusting him, so he can ride into town with us and we'll talk to Frank Lyle about him. If Lyle trusts him then so shall we. I'm thinking about making some changes in our set-up, and mebbe this feller can help.'

'You set too much store by Lyle,' Tate replied. 'It was his word that put Braska in here running the gun crew, and he's another I don't trust any further than I could throw him with one hand tied behind my back.'

'You'll ride into town with us?' Farron's gaze bored into Jordan.

'I've just ridden out from Oak Bend and it ain't a place I'd wanta return to.' Jordan's tone was obdurate.

'What kind of an answer is that?'

Farron frowned. 'You rode in here asking for a job.'

'I ain't hired yet. When I am then you can give me orders.'

'Where have you worked before?' Tate rapped.

'You wouldn't know anything more about me if I told you,' Jordan countered, wondering which of these two had ordered the shots to be fired that had wounded his father and brother.

Tate sighed impatiently. 'What the hell is this? Why don't I just shoot him and have done with it? What for are you wasting time on him, Abel?'

'You're taking a lot for granted if you reckon you can take care of me,' Jordan challenged.

Tate's narrowed eyes flamed and he drew a deep breath. Colour came into his face and his lips pulled into a tight, uncompromising line.

'The hell with it,' he rasped, and reached for his pistol, his gun hand moving in a blur of speed.

Jordan moved simultaneously, set into motion by the signal of intention that appeared in Tate's eyes. His pistol appeared in his hand, and the three clicks of it being cocked sounded before Tate could clear leather. Tate froze when he saw the black muzzle gaping at him, and instinctively thrust his weapon back into its holster and released the butt. A pang of cold fear struck through his chest and his mouth gaped. Abel Farron remained motionless, but a tight grin appeared on his lips and his eyes glinted.

'Looks like you overplayed your hand this time, Sam,' Farron observed drily. 'With a draw like that, I reckon we can't afford not to use this guy.'

'Maybe I don't wanta work with a ramrod who is dead set against me,' Jordan mused. 'He'll be wondering if my draw was a fluke, and might be forced to try me out again. It would be better to get that over with now.' He holstered his gun with a slick movement and let his hand hover above the butt.

'Care to try it again?' he offered. 'This time I'll go all the way.'

Tate shook his head. 'The hell I do! I'll get ready for that trip into town, Abel.' He turned away, saying, 'You're the boss, Abel, and if you wanta take this bozo on then it's no skin off my nose.'

Farron grinned as he watched the big ramrod stalk across the yard, shoulders stiff and head high.

'Tate ain't gonna forgive you for bracing him,' Farron opined. 'He'll take up your challenge soon as he figures he's got an edge. You got gun speed, but are you ready to kill on order?'

'Sure. You got killers on your payroll and they're getting away with murder. You reckon to have the local law in your pocket. Who shot Saul Jordan and his son Lance? Are you planning to take over Box J?'

'You ask too many questions, mister.' Farron's eyes narrowed.

'A man needs to know what he's getting into if he takes a job with an outfit like yours.' Jordan smiled coldly.

'Is that so?'

Farron suppressed a shiver as he gazed at Jordan, sensing an imperceptible change in Jordan's attitude as Tate drew further away across the yard. He saw deadly intention in Jordan's hard gaze and moved his hand towards his left armpit.

'You got a strange manner for a man seeking a job,' he observed.

'I don't want a job.' Jordan shook his head. 'In fact, I already got one. I'm on the payroll at Box J, and I rode in here to see what kind of a man you really are. Well, I can tell you are hell-bent on your crooked business and nothing short of a slug will stop you. I don't like you, Farron, and it'll please me to fight you. Most of the men you sent out this morning to attack Box J are dead, Ritson is dead, and Braska is on his way into town as a prisoner. How'd you like that?'

Farron was shocked speechless. His face paled and he gazed at Jordan as if his worst nightmare had come true.

'You better take out that gun in your shoulder holster before you make the mistake of trying to use it,' Jordan said softly. 'I'd like nothing better than to put you down right now.'

'You got gall, riding in here with my crew around.' Farron looked towards the guard at the gate, and then directed his gaze towards the corrals, where several men were standing.

'They could be on the moon for all the help any of them can give you right now,' Jordan observed. 'What's it feel like to know you're standing on the edge of hell? You've been throwing your weight around this range, and I suppose I'll have to kill you in the end, but you might be able to save yourself by pulling in your horns around Box J. Just one more incident involving any of the Jordans and you're as good as dead. Is that clear?'

'You think you can get away with this?' Farron snarled.

'It sure looks like I can,' Jordan responded.

'Hell, I only got to snap my fingers and twenty men will be on your trail. Real killers, too, who won't give a second thought about putting out your light.'

'That would be a real mistake.' Jordan saw Sam Tate harnessing a horse to a buggy and knew the ramrod would soon be returning to the house. 'Try it and see how many of your hardcases come home. Now disarm yourself, and don't make any mistake about that. Get rid of your hardware, Farron, and count yourself lucky I'm giving you a chance to straighten out your play.'

Farron grasped the butt of his holstered pistol and drew the weapon into the open, using thumb and forefinger only. He paused with the weapon dangling, and Jordan laughed.

'Go ahead, if you think you can do it,' he invited. 'I'll match you.'

Farron exhaled and relaxed his hand, allowing the pistol to thump on the boards of the porch. He kicked the weapon into the dust of the yard and dropped his hands to his sides.

'Walk along the porch to the far end,' Jordan ordered. 'I'm riding out now, and you better stay quiet until I'm in the clear or I'll come back and gutshoot you.'

Farron obeyed. Jordan took up his reins and walked to the end of the porch. Farron gazed at him wordlessly.

'Get off the porch and walk around the side of the house with me,' Jordan said. He stepped up into his saddle as Farron obeyed and they continued towards the rear of the house. 'I'll be seeing you again, no doubt,' Jordan commented, touching spurs to his horse, and set off at a lope from the house.

He kept an eye on Farron as he departed, expecting the rancher to hurry back to the porch for his gun, but Farron remained motionless, watching his departure, and Jordan continued until he cleared a rise and the house was lost to sight. Dismounting, he drew his long gun, dropped flat and crawled back up to the skyline, where he awaited pursuit.

Farron returned to the porch, moving unhurriedly, and disappeared from sight around the corner. A few moments later a pistol hammered three times, and Jordan grinned as he awaited a reaction. Pretty soon now he would be knee-deep in hardcases.

Minutes later six riders came galloping around a corner of the house. Jordan jacked a shell into the breech of his Winchester as they approached. He shot the foremost rider in the chest and then quickly shifted his aim to send a stream of 44.40 slugs into the thick of the advancing group. The flat crack of the shooting tore across the ranch and reverberated into the distance.

Pandemonium flared among the riders. Three of them vacated their saddles and lay still on the dusty ground. The remaining three wheeled their mounts and hurriedly sought cover in front of the house. Jordan eased back, slid his smoking rifle into its saddle boot and regained his saddle. He rode out fast, keeping an eye on his back trail, grimly satisfied with his morning's work.

He covered a couple of miles in the general direction of Oak Bend and then dismounted again to lie up in good cover and watch for further pursuit. He remained motionless for thirty minutes, and then decided there was no pursuit. He had given Farron something to think about, showing up at the spread alone and acting so brazenly in asking for a job. It had been a good start to his campaign, he thought, but he now had to follow it up, had to top it with a battle-winning scoop that would give him a better than fifty per cent chance of besting Farron.

He arose to continue to Oak Bend, hot and dusty, and ready for more action . . .

Oak Bend lay baking in the glare of the sun. The town consisted of just one wide street running north to south. There was one hotel, Puma House, its woodwork badly in need of a coat of paint. The bank was built of brick, as were the law office and jail, and the rest of the buildings straggling along on either side of the thoroughfare were made of wood, unlovely in the sunlight.

Jordan remembered the town well from his boyhood, and sat his horse at the north end of the street, his keen gaze picking out the places he had known. Dawson's saloon was three doors down from the store, and a couple of saddle-horses were standing hip-shot at the tie-rail outside. There was a buckboard in front of Wacey's store, and a man and a woman were carrying supplies out of the store and loading them in the vehicle. The scene looked so very peaceful, but Jordan was not deceived by the atmosphere.

The bank held Jordan's gaze, for it was on the boardwalk outside its door that his mother had bled to death before they could get the doctor to her. His gaze flickered to the law office as he touched spurs to the flanks of his horse and moved into the street. The first thing he had to do was brace Frank Lyle, the deputy who, by all accounts, was in Abel Farron's pocket. He assumed that his father and brother would be in the hotel by now, and hoped Hester was staying out of sight. He needed to see Sheriff Holder, if possible, to discover the nature of the situation existing in the town.

He dismounted outside the law office and wrapped his reins around the tie-rail there. The silence was overpowering as he stamped on to the boardwalk and opened the office door. The interior was dim and he paused for a couple of moments for his eyes to become adjusted, then entered and closed the door noisily. His right hand was close to the butt of his gun.

A man was seated at the desk facing the door, apparently asleep, for both his arms were on the desk and his head was resting on them. The slamming door jerked him awake and he sat up with a start, rubbing his eyes. Jordan wondered who he was. He could not be

Frank Lyle because he was no more than a youth, and, when he got to his feet, Jordan could see that he was unarmed.

'Sorry to wake you,' Jordan said. 'Is the sheriff around?'

'Nope. He's on night duty these days. Frank Lyle is the deputy sheriff and he's around during the day. I'm Danny Baer, the jailer.'

'So where is Lyle?'

'Somewhere around town. He was busy this morning. The Jordans rode in from Box J earlier. They brought Jingle Bob Jones, their ranch foreman. He'd been shot and is at the doc's place now. They had Braska, one of Farron's outfits, hogtied as a prisoner, and wanted to put him behind bars.'

'Have you got Braska locked up?' Jordan enquired.

Baer laughed and shook his head. 'You gotta be joking! Lyle sent the Jordans packing with a warning to get out of town. Him and Braska went along to the saloon for a drink, and as far as I know they're still there.'

'What did the Jordans do?'

'They took Jingle Bob to the doc's office. I ain't seen them since, but if they got any sense at all they'll make themselves scarce. This is Farron's town, and there's trouble between the Jordans and Farron so I reckon their days are numbered.'

Jordan nodded and turned to leave. He paused at the door.

'I'll look up Lyle,' he said, and departed.

Jordan's thoughts were harsh as he traversed the boardwalk. Despite his crooked association with Farron, Lyle was a lawman, and there was no way he could be killed with impunity. But Jordan's steps did not waver and he went along to the saloon and looked in over the batwings. The place was deserted apart from a man behind the bar, who was busy washing glasses. He looked up when Jordan entered. The silence was overpowering, almost tangible, and Jordan's boots rapped the pine floor as he crossed to the bar.

'What'll it be, stranger?' the bartender demanded.

'Beer,' Jordan responded, and reached into his pocket for a coin.

A tall glass slid before him and he picked it up and drank deeply before licking his lips. The tender watched him intently, smiling.

'I'm looking for Frank Lyle,' Jordan said.

The bartender's smile vanished and he shook his head. 'He was here earlier — came in with a feller named Braska. They had a beer and then left. I heard a ruckus outside just after that — voices, one of them being the Jordan gal. Then there was silence, and I ain't seen hide nor hair of Lyle after that.'

'I'll find him.' Jordan finished his beer and departed.

He paused outside to look around, and then went on to the hotel, watching his surroundings closely. The street was deserted and he wondered at the lack of folk going about their daily business.

He stepped into the dusty lobby and paused to take stock. A clerk was sitting behind the reception desk, reading a newspaper. He did not look up when Jordan paused at the desk.

'Are the Jordans booked in here?'

The clerk looked up, apparently irritated by Jordan's intrusion. He shrugged and returned his attention to the newspaper.

'I asked you a question.' Jordan stared at the man. 'Have you lost your tongue?'

'Mister, nobody talks about the Jordans in this town. Leave me be.'

Jordan reached over the desk, grasped the man by the scruff of his neck and hauled him across the desk. Setting him on his feet, he grasped a handful of his shirt front and held him steady.

'I won't repeat the question because you've heard it, so give me an answer now.'

'I've been warned not to talk about the Jordans,' the clerk countered.

'Who warned you?' Jordan rasped.

'I did,' a voice said from across the lobby.

Jordan glanced to his left to see a tall, thin man standing in the arch that led into the small dining room. He was holding a levelled pistol in his right hand, and there was a deputy sheriff law star pinned to his shirt.

'You'll be Frank Lyle,' Jordan said instantly. 'Abel Farron sent me in with a message.'

He paused, smiling, to see how Lyle would take his bluff.

5

'I ain't seen you around before.' Lyle's cold blue eyes were glistening. He waggled his pistol. 'Let go of Edlin. Everyone around here does what they're told, and know they don't talk about the Jordans. What's the message from Farron?'

Jordan released the clerk and the man scuttled away.

'Farron says to tell you Braska and some of the outfit set out to do a job at dawn and didn't ride back to Rafter F. He wants you to check the town for them, and if they're here you gotta boot them back to where they came from.'

'They ain't here.' Lyle holstered his gun but did not relax. 'Most of them were killed by a gunnie Hester Jordan hired. Braska was here, and told me this new guy is hell on wheels. I'm looking forward to meeting up with him.'

'What happened to the Jordans? They came into town, huh?'

'I sent them back to their spread. They ain't welcome in town.'

'And Braska? Where's he gone?'

'Rode out to Flying D with a message for Two-Finger Dack before swinging back to Rafter F. He's a mite shook up by what happened at Box J.' Lyle grinned. 'I told him if he's scared of the new gunnie then he better round up a few men and dry-gulch him. Farron is paying good wages for top gunhands, but he ain't getting top service.'

Jordan could tell the kind of man Lyle was — typical of the type who sold gun service to the highest bidder — cold and merciless. He wanted to challenge the man to fight, but was too keenly aware that the law star glinting on Lyle's shirt made such an action impossible to win. If he killed Lyle he would be branded an outlaw.

'I'd better be heading back to Farron,' Jordan said.

Lyle grinned. 'Let's have a drink before you sift outa here. Farron can wait.'

'Nope. I got to be getting back. I'm gonna do what I get paid for, which ain't standing around here.'

Jordan moved towards the street door, and did not turn his back to the killer deputy. He stepped out to the boardwalk, looking back at Lyle, and at that instant the hard muzzle of a pistol jabbed against his spine. He froze in mid-action, still looking at Lyle, and saw a hard grin appear on the man's thin lips.

'Got you dead to rights,' said the man with the gun. 'Don't move a muscle.'

Jordan recognized Braska's voice and remained motionless. He felt a hand snatch his pistol from its holster. Lyle came in close.

'Figured you were too smart for us, huh?' Lyle said. 'If Braska hadn't described you then I guess I might have been fooled at that. It's a good thing you stuck around, Braska. You didn't exaggerate when you said this guy is smarter than a wagonload of monkeys. But he's come to the end of his trail now. You can take him out to Farron and see what the boss makes of him. Don't let him get away from you.'

'I ain't herding him out to Rafter F,' Braska protested. 'Lock him in your jail until Farron tells you what to do with him. I need to travel fast. Farron will want to change his orders about the Jordans after what happened at Box J this morning. I reckon he'll want the whole bunch of them dead and buried.'

'OK. But make it quick. I don't want this guy in my jail any longer than is necessary.' Turning to Jordan, Lyle said, 'On your way, mister. The jail is to the right.'

Jordan walked to the law office, covered by two pistols, and frustration simmered in him at his change of fortune, aware now that he should have ridden out of town the instant he learned his family had departed. First and foremost, he had to ensure their safety, but here he was in the hands of his enemies with little chance of escape. He had disobeyed the first rule of his job.

Lyle made Jordan turn out his pockets and, with Braska still covering him, led the way into the cell block. Jordan entered a cell and the iron door clanged shut, sounding like the knell of doom in his ears. Lyle locked the door with a flourish. His evil face was alive with malice.

'You didn't last long, mister,' he said. 'Farron will want you dead when he learns how you killed his gunnies.'

Braska and Lyle departed into the office and Jordan prowled around the small cell like a caged tiger. He shook the cell door, such was his frustration, and then accepted his change of fortune and sat down on the bunk. He had to escape from this situation, and his mind teemed with possibilities.

Aware that he could do nothing until

Lyle revisited him, or Braska returned from Rafter F with fresh orders, Jordan stretched out on the bunk, tipped his hat over his eyes, and tried to sleep away the time. He did not think he would be successful, but was awakened by the crash of the connecting door between office and cells being thrown open. He sat up, and was surprised to discover that daylight was fading and several hours had passed since he was jailed.

The jailer appeared, accompanied by an older man, and Jordan arose from the bunk and went to the cell door. It took him more than a first glance to recognize the older man as the sheriff, Jake Holder, and he was surprised that the last ten years had taken such a great toll on the law man. Holder was about fifty, but looked ten years older. His hair was grey, his shoulders stooped. His face was wrinkled and seamed, and he looked to be a faded version of the man Jordan had known. He looked like a man who should be spending his time sitting in the sun instead of toting a law star.

Holder came to the door of the cell and peered at Jordan. Recognition showed in his narrowed brown eyes and he nodded.

'OK, Danny,' he said to the youthful jailer. 'I'll have a chat with the prisoner. You go off duty now. I'll take over.'

Danny Baer handed over the cell keys and departed readily. Holder heaved a sigh. He waited until he heard the street door slam behind the departing jailer and then hung the ring containing the keys over the butt of his holstered gun.

'You've grown up some since I last saw you, Travis,' Holder said, and there was a trace of weariness in his voice. 'Hester came and saw me when she got into town before noon. She told me you were back in the county and how you tore into Farron's gunnies. She wanted me to help you, but I told her I'm too old. I hate to admit it, but I'm past it now, son. I can't stand up to these hard-cases any more. Lyle is a cold-blooded killer. He's got me running scared. Will ya look at me? I come in here as night jailer instead of handling my normal duties because Lyle is cracking the whip these days.'

'I should have killed Lyle when I rode in,' Jordan said. 'The only thing that stopped me was the law star he's wearing.'

'He's wearing a badge but he ain't a lawful deputy, Travis. He took that badge off my desk the day Farron sent him into town to handle things around here, and I never swore him in. He's just a killer hiding behind a badge.'

Jordan gripped the bars of the cell door.

'I wish I'd known that when I rode into town,' he gritted between his teeth. 'Let me out, Sheriff, and I'll take that badge off him. Lyle sent Hester and the family back to the ranch, and they were attacked there this morning. I'm afraid Farron will send more men to finish them off. I need to get out to Box J soon as I can.'

'I'd like to help you, Travis, but Lyle

would kill me if I stepped out of line.' The sheriff shook his head wearily.

'He won't be around long enough to kill anyone,' Jordan said tensely. 'Turn me loose and stay here while I go for him.'

Holder shook his head again. His hands were trembling and his face was pale with the tension gripping him.

'I can't do that,' he said apologetically. 'I'm too far down the hill to make a stand.' He took the keys off his gun butt and dropped them to the floor, then kicked them in close to the bars. 'But you could let yourself out when I'm in the front office, huh?' He grinned. 'Then come through and pick up your gun. I took the trouble of going along to the stable and saddling up your horse before I came on duty. That'll save you some time. When you get out, it's up to you what you do about Lyle, but he's mighty fast with a gun.'

'Thanks, Sheriff.' Jordan reached between the bars and gripped Holder's hand. 'All I need is one small break and your troubles will be over.'

The sheriff smiled sadly and turned away. Jordan reached between the bars and snatched up the bunch of keys. Urgency gripped him as he fumbled the biggest key of the bunch into the lock on the door. Twisting it, he heard the click of the lock, and the door swung open instantly. He hurried out of the cell after Holder, and found the sheriff standing in the front office.

'Is this your gun?' Holder demanded, holding out a holstered pistol in a cartridge belt.

Jordan grasped the weapon, checked it quickly, and changed the loads in the cylinder. He holstered the gun and then swung the heavy belt around his waist and buckled it, feeling relief at its familiar weight on his right hip.

'Lyle will be in the café at this time of the evening,' Holder said.

'Thanks, Sheriff. I'll look him up now.'

'Just watch yourself, son,' Holder

advised. 'Before you go, there's one thing I can do for you.' He opened a desk drawer, produced a law star and held it out. 'Pin this on your shirt and raise your right hand. I'll swear you in as a deputy. That'll protect you against any comeback if you kill Lyle.'

Jordan nodded, pinned the star to his shirt and, as he raised his right hand, the street door was thrust open and a large, middle-aged man entered the office. He hesitated on the threshold when he found himself looking into the muzzle of Jordan's gun.

'What's going on?' he demanded, startled.

'It's OK, Henry,' Holder replied. 'This is Travis Jordan. Remember him? He's Saul Jordan's eldest son come back to fight Farron. Travis, this is Henry Forder — owns the hotel, and he's the town mayor. I was about to swear Travis in as a deputy, Henry. I'll be with you in a moment.'

When the swearing-in process was over Jordan departed quickly, slipping out to the sidewalk. He was immediately encompassed by shadows, and sighed heavily to rid himself of mounting tension. Lyle now fully occupied his thoughts, but he was aware, in the back of his mind, that Braska had had time to get to Farron and then return with an armed party either to kill him out of hand or haul him out to Rafter F.

Jordan stepped into the street and moved silently towards the café, flexing the fingers of his right hand. The last traces of daylight were lingering in the western sky and yellow lamplight flared from windows along the street. Deep silence enveloped the town, broken only by the muted sounds of a piano being played in the big saloon. There were a few passers-by on the sidewalks, anonymous in the darkness.

He paused at the big window of the café and peered inside. The evening rush was over. Two waitresses were busy clearing up and only three men were seated at the tables — one of them

Frank Lyle. The killer was sitting at his ease, smoking a cigarette and reading a newspaper, the star on his shirt glinting in the lamplight.

Jordan opened the door of the café and stepped inside. Lyle looked up at the sound of his entry. He frowned at the sight of Jordan's big figure, and then his expression filled with shock as recognition dawned. He started to his feet, overturning his chair in his haste. The cigarette fell from his lips. His right hand flashed to his holstered gun. The weapon cleared its holster in a blur of speed, but Jordan, moving simultaneously, had drawn and cocked his pistol before the killer could get his gun into action.

Jordan squeezed his trigger and the blasting explosion of the shot ripped out the silence, its power rocking the diner, making stacked plates rattle. Lyle took the bullet in his chest and was flung backwards by the impact. His pistol fell from his hand and blood spread over his shirt front as he pitched to the floor, flattening a table in the process.

A waitress nearby stood frozen, a hand to her mouth in shock, her eyes wide. Two male diners were transfixed, staring at Lyle's body as if trying to believe the evidence of their goggling eyes.

The fading echoes of the shot had set up a buzzing in Jordan's ears, and he swallowed to clear them. He went forward to stand over Lyle, and did not need a second glance to see that the man was dead. He holstered his gun, and then turned swiftly as the street door was opened, his pistol reappearing in his deadly hand. Sheriff Holder entered, followed closely by Henry Forder, and came to Jordan's side. Holder gazed silently at Lyle.

'You beat him!' he rasped in a trembling tone. 'You killed him, Travis. No more Frank Lyle! He ruled this town like a tyrant, and it looked like no one could pull him down. He murdered more than a dozen men, and all in the name of the law. Travis, you better get out of here now. When Farron learns of this he's gonna turn out his entire outfit to get you. He'll figure you are too dangerous to be allowed to live. He can set twenty men out after you, and they wouldn't give you a dog's chance.'

'I'm gonna fetch my family back into town and then I'm heading out to Rafter F to nail Farron,' Jordan said quietly. 'Or I'll be here waiting for the showdown when he shows up. He doesn't know it yet but his reign is over.'

'I'll gather a posse by the time you come back,' Holder said with sudden enthusiasm. 'If we can put Farron on trial we'll break the back of the trouble round here. You've given me fresh hope, Travis.'

'Bring your family to the hotel when you get back from Box J, Travis.' Forder's dark eyes were bright, filled with calculation. 'I'll see that nothing happens to them while you're after Farron.'

'Thanks.' Jordan departed, filled with concern for his family.

He found his horse ready-saddled in the livery barn and rode out fast, following the trail to Box J. The night was silent and still. Stars were already twinkling remotely in the wide sky, and a half-moon showed in the east, just above the distant horizon. A keen breeze blew into his face and he breathed deeply, pushing his horse along at a fast pace, the sound of rattling hoofs on the hard trail echoing urgently.

As he approached Box J, Jordan was relieved to see lights showing peacefully in the ranch house. He had feared that he would be too late and would find a gang of rustlers shooting up the spread. He rode in openly, expecting a guard to be on duty, and a voice called to him from dense shadow as he approached the gate. He shouted a reply and Charlie Pierce emerged from cover with a steady rifle.

'We had trouble in town,' Pierce said

when he recognized Jordan.

'I heard about it,' Jordan replied. 'I've just come from there. Has there been any trouble here?'

'Nary a thing since we got back, and I'm a mite worried because it's been so quiet. It ain't like Farron to miss any chances, and I've been expecting Braska or Lyle to come out here with some hardcases to finish us off.'

'Lyle is dead.' Jordan glanced around into the surrounding shadows. 'I'm the new deputy.'

'You killed Lyle?' Pierce let out a yell that echoed across the yard.

'What in hell is going on?' a voice called from the shadows on the porch of the house. 'Are you drunk, Charlie?'

'Get the buckboard saddled up and we'll take the family back into town,' Jordan directed, and Pierce hurried away to the corral.

Jordan rode up to the house and came under the ready muzzle of Tom Baldwin's long gun.

'What was Charlie celebrating?'

Baldwin demanded when he recognized Jordan, and yelled in delight when Jordan explained.

'Heck, I'd have given a month's pay to see that event,' he declared. 'Gimme all the gory details.'

'Later. We're heading back to town now. Once the family is safe I'm gonna take the war to Farron and that'll mean hard riding and fast shooting. Charlie is bringing the buckboard. I'll get the family prepared to move out. This is a dangerous spot to be in right now.'

The door of the house was standing open and Hester appeared in the doorway, attracted by the shouts, and she was perfectly silhouetted by the flaring lamplight. Jordan cringed. If Farron's crew rode in now there would be mayhem. He went forward quickly.

'Travis, I've been so worried about you!' Hester exclaimed. 'I've been expecting trouble ever since we returned. Lyle wouldn't let us stay in town, and I know what was in his mind when he chased us out. Where have you been? I was thinking all kinds of bad things had happened to you.'

'You shouldn't have come back here, and I'm taking you back to Oak Bend,' Jordan said. 'Don't waste time, Hester. Get Dad and Lance ready. Charlie is bringing the buckboard and you're moving out.'

'But Lyle will only run us out again,' Hester protested.

'Lyle is dead.' Jordan turned so that lamplight fell upon his chest.

Hester gasped when she saw the deputy star pinned on him, and raised a hand to her mouth in horror as Jordan recounted the events that had occurred in town.

'Don't look so shocked.' He smiled grimly. 'You must have known what would happen when you came to Texas for me. This is the only way I know of fighting a man like Farron so do like I say and get ready to move out. I'm surprised Farron hasn't struck at you before this. When you get to town, see Sheriff Holder, and he'll put you into the hotel, where Forder has said he'll keep an eye on you.'

'And what are you going to do?' Hester demanded.

'What I came home for.' Jordan moved impatiently. 'Hurry it along, Hester. I want to be here alone when a bunch of Farron's hardcases show up. I'm surprised they haven't showed already.'

Hester hurried into the house and Jordan stood in the shadows on the porch between the window and the door, peering into the night, his ears strained for the first ominous sound of approaching horses. The silence of the range mocked him, but he was thankful for the respite and, by the time the buckboard came across the yard, Hester was standing on the porch with Saul and Lance.

'Travis, let me stay here with you,' Lance protested.

'Do you really want to help me?' Jordan countered.

'Sure thing. Tell me what to do.'

'Just do like I tell you. Go into town with Hester and Dad, and be ready to defend them if the need arises.'

'OK.' Lance shook his head and climbed into the buckboard. 'I thought I could be more help here.'

'I need to be here alone when trouble strikes.' Jordan looked around into the shadows. His ears were strained and he was thankful he could hear nothing beyond the natural night noises of the surrounding range.

His relief increased when the vehicle pulled out. Hester was driving the team with Pierce and Baldwin riding behind on their saddle-horses. Both cowboys would stay in town guarding the family. Jordan stood on the porch listening intently until the sound of grating wheels faded and an uneasy silence settled over the deserted spread. Then he entered the house and turned out the lamps. He stood in the darkness, his thoughts flitting back over the distant past, when he had lived here and his mother had been alive.

He moved out within thirty minutes and found cover on a knoll overlooking the yard at a distance of almost one hundred yards. He left his horse saddled and knee-hobbled, spread his blanket roll on the hard ground and turned in to get some sleep, his pistol in his right hand. The moon changed its position in the night sky, and he was awakened, as dawn sneaked into the eastern sky, by the beat and thud of approaching hoofs.

By the time the dim figures of six riders entered the yard, Jordan was ready with his rifle and pistol. He watched the men cross the yard. Daylight was strengthening with each passing moment. The barn looked ghostly in the grey light of dawn. Jordan jacked a shell into the breech of his Winchester, and the metallic sounds were harsh in the natural silence. When three of the riders dismounted and trailed their reins, Jordan lifted his rifle into the aim. The waiting was over. His family was safely out of it and he could wage war on his own terms.

Two of the newcomers struck matches and ignited brands which they carried. Jordan did not care if they burned the house because it could be rebuilt, but as two of the men stepped up on to the porch he shattered the brooding silence with carefully aimed shots.

6

The rifle recoiled in Jordan's steady hands and kicked against his right shoulder. The flat crack of two shots echoed away into the vast distance. The two men on the porch buckled instantly and pitched to the sun-warped boards, writhing and kicking. The remaining four riders wheeled their mounts and began shooting at shadows. Jordan fired at them mercilessly. Two of their number pitched from their saddles and the surviving two swung away to gallop for the nearest corner of the house, seeking cover. Jordan shot another, and was just too late to nail the surviving rider, who disappeared around the corner and kept riding fast.

Jordan reloaded and lay watching the yard. One of the downed men was moving jerkily but the others were inert. He had shot to kill. These men were gun wolves — men who sold their lives for dollars, and they had come here to kill innocent, hard-working folk. They were range vermin, and he felt no emotion at ending their useless lives.

He got to his feet when he was satisfied that no further attack was coming. The sun was clearing the eastern horizon now, and the shadows had fled. He prepared his horse for travel and stepped up into the saddle to take out after the surviving rider. Hoof prints were clear in the dust and he rode fast, wanting to press home his advantage. He needed to get to Oak Bend as soon as possible, but first he had a chore to handle.

The tracks led him straight to Rafter F, and two hours later he was sitting his horse on a ridge overlooking Farron's spread and studying the layout. There were signs of great activity in and around the yard. He counted more than twenty horses saddled and ready to ride, and a large group of men were gathered in front of the porch, upon which two men were standing.

Jordan recognized the diminutive figure of Abel Farron and the larger shape of Sam Tate, the ranch foreman, on the porch. Farron was waving his hands as he spoke, and it was obvious that fighting orders were being issued. Jordan drew his Winchester, adjusted his sights, and dismounted. He led his horse back into full cover and then dropped to the ground and crawled forward until he had a clear view of the yard.

He peered through his sights and centred upon Farron, allowed for the steady breeze, and fired. Farron jumped as if he had been kicked by a mule. He spun, fell heavily on the porch, and then squirmed around and crawled jerkily into the house through the open doorway, using his elbows and knees desperately. Jordan jacked a fresh shell into his breech as the echoes of the shot hammered away. Pandemonium broke out among the tightly grouped men. They broke and ran for cover, pulling guns and looking around for a target. Tate turned to enter the house but Jordan drew a bead on the big ramrod and fired again.

Tate sprawled untidily on the porch and lay inert. Jordan turned his attention to the running gunhands, and his deadly rifle crackled as he sent a stream of .44.40 slugs into their ranks. Four men hit the dust and lay still before the rest found cover. Jordan withdrew from his vantage point and went back to his horse. He needed to get to town, collect a posse, and return to take advantage of his grim success.

He rode out with his rifle across his thighs, keeping an eye on his back trail. He did not expect immediate pursuit because he had nailed both Farron and Tate, and there was no one left at the ranch to give orders. He angled into the west and rode steadily, a breeze blowing into his face, and, when he caught the tang of smoke, he moved forward carefully until he topped a rise and saw three men in the middle-distance.

They were grouped around a small fire. Jordan quickened his pace. It looked, at first glance, as if he had come across rustlers in the act of their lawlessness.

A steer had been roped and thrown close to the fire and one of the men was sitting on the animal's head. A man was approaching the fallen steer with a hot running iron in his hand. Jordan rode in closer, and the men were alerted by the sound of approaching hoofs. They swung around, spotted Jordan, and reached for their holstered guns.

Jordan was aware that he was still on Box J, slid his rifle into its boot and drew his pistol. The trio at the fire began to shoot at him, and he heard a slug crackle over his head as he returned fire.

His first shot struck the man holding the running iron and dumped him on his face across the fire. Jordan cut loose then, aiming and shooting, and did not hear the sound of anything coming back at him. His second shot caused one of the surviving men to drop his pistol and turn to run towards the spot where three horses were standing.

Jordan triggered the Colt, saw the third man waver, and fired again. The man went down and Jordan rode in fast. The second man managed to get mounted, but Jordan was upon him before he could spur his horse.

'Hold it,' Jordan shouted.

The man cast a quick glance in Jordan's direction, realized that he could not get clear, and reached for his pistol. Jordan thumbed off a shot and the man slid out of his saddle. Echoes faded sullenly across the range. Jordan reined in and stepped down. He dragged the man off the fire, and then took stock of the situation.

All three men were dead, and there was nothing in their pockets or saddle-bags to identify them. He saw that each of their horses was carrying the Rafter F brand — a large F with a sloping line over it — and did not need further proof of what had been going on. When he checked the gather of twelve steers standing close by he saw that the Box J brand on them had been altered with a running iron.

This was all the evidence he needed to prove rustling against Farron's ranch, and he was grimly satisfied. He straightened, checked his surroundings, and a movement off along his back trail jolted him back to reality. He was being tracked. He saw eight men appear on a ridge, and the next instant they were firing rapidly at him.

Jordan grimaced as he regained his saddle. He sent the big horse on fast, angling for the distant town, and the riders came along behind. He had taught them to respect his gun prowess for they stayed just out of effective rifle range. When he had pulled clear he looked for an ambush spot, and finally hunkered down on a ridge with his rifle at the ready.

His pursuers might be thinking that they had got him on the run, but he intended to teach them the art of fighting on the move and waited patiently for them to draw within range. Four riders appeared and came forward steadily, and Jordan searched his surroundings for signs of the others. He caught a glimpse of a rider on a skyline to his right and guessed they were trying to circle around him.

He waited until the riders were clear of any cover before lifting his rifle. His foresight covered the chest of the leading man. He squeezed the trigger and the man slumped in his saddle. The remaining three riders spurred rapidly for other parts, and Jordan picked off two more of them and barely missed the third as the man hammered over a ridge and was lost to sight.

Jordan went back to his horse and rode back along his trail, passing the dead Farron men on the ground. He angled to the right and circled fast, cutting across the tracks left by the four men who were trying to get around him. He followed grimly until he crossed a rise and saw them in the middle-distance. They were sitting their mounts and looking around, nervous as a class of Sunday-school children.

Jordan checked his weapons and then went forward at a run He was not spotted until he started shooting, and by then he was comfortably in range and his bullets began to find their targets.

Two riders hit the dust and the remaining pair took off at a gallop and looked as if they would not stop this side of the border. Jordan resumed his ride, watching his surroundings closely, and the sun had passed its zenith when he saw Oak Bend sprawling in the distance. He checked his back trail, but if there were hostile riders behind him then they were keeping at a respectful distance.

Jordan rode to the entrance of the single street and reined in. There was no movement anywhere — no horses at tie-rails, no folk outside buildings, and no dogs lazing in the sun. Silence was heavy, and the stillness gave Jordan the thought that this was a ghost town. A pang struck through him as he moved on. His family should be here now, and he needed to check with Hester before he did anything else.

He rode on to the law office and dismounted wearily, wrapping his reins around the tie-rail. He glanced around the deserted street, frowning at the emptiness, and questions began piling up in his mind as he turned to the office. He pulled up abruptly when the door failed to open, and shook it, discovering it was locked. His right hand dropped to the butt of his holstered pistol as he turned his back to it and once more surveyed the street.

A man emerged from the store and ran across the street without looking left or right to vanish into a shop opposite. The door slammed echoingly behind him. Jordan began to feel as if he had walked into a trap. His sixth sense was suddenly working overtime and he could not ignore the warning flashing in his mind. Something had gone wrong.

He walked along the boardwalk, checking his surroundings every step of the way, intending to go to the hotel to see Hester. When he reached the open doorway of the general store he paused and glanced inside. The place was deserted. He gazed into the interior for long moments before going on, and there was a tingling sensation between his shoulder blades as he continued.

'Get off the street!' a voice yelled suddenly. 'The town is staked out by gunnies.'

Jordan moved without thinking. He dived sideways into the nearest door-way, which happened to be the bank, and a gun fired from somewhere across the street. A bullet thudded into the doorpost only an inch from his head. He drew his gun as he turned, and saw a puff of black gun smoke hazing from an alley mouth opposite. His finger trembled on his trigger, but there was no target to shoot at.

Tense moments passed, and then three figures emerged from the alley and came across the street. Jordan recognized Braska among them and cocked his pistol. The three men were holding pistols but made no attempt to fire. Jordan's mouth pulled into a grimace when he spotted a law star on Braska's shirt front.

'Jordan, listen to me,' Braska called. 'I got your family under guard, and if you don't toe the line they'll die pronto. Come on out without your gun and we'll talk about this.'

'Where's the sheriff?' Jordan countered, resisting the urge to open fire.

'He left town for the benefit of his health.' Braska was grinning, sure of himself in this situation, and he lifted his left hand to brush his thumb over the glinting star on his shirt front. 'Holder left me in charge of the law.'

'That ain't strictly true,' a voice said behind Jordan. 'Braska ran Holder out — at least I think he did. I ain't seen the sheriff since Braska rode into town with those two thugs and they took Holder along the street to the livery barn.'

Jordan glanced over his shoulder to see a tall, thin man standing beside the big window in the front wall where he could watch the street, and recognized Benton Deane, the banker, who was holding a shotgun in his hands.

'I spoke to Holder this morning before Braska turned up,' Deane continued, 'and he told me he deputized you before you shot Lyle. It looked like our troubles were over, and then Braska showed up. Farron was quick to replace Lyle, and now he's got a real stranglehold on the town. I saw Hester arrive with Saul, Lance and two cowboys, and Braska and those gunnies with him shot the cowboys and then took your family off along the street at gunpoint.'

'You've had time to think this over,' Braska called. 'Come out with your hands up or it'll go bad with your family.'

'Is there a back door to this place?' Jordan asked.

'Sure.' Deane indicated a door in the

back wall of the office. 'Through there. A door leads out to the back lots.'

Jordan moved fast. He had no alternative, aware that if he obeyed Braska's command he would place himself in an impossible position. He left the bank by the rear door and started along the back lots at a run, heading for the livery barn, certain that Braska would not have sent Sheriff Holder out of town. He was breathless when he entered the barn.

The light was dim inside the dusty stable, and Jordan paused to accustom his eyes to the shadows. A horse stamped somewhere, the noise startling him, and he walked through the barn with his finger trembling on the trigger of his pistol. Beams of bright yellow sunlight shafted through gaps between the warped boards and dazzled him. A figure was standing in a stall near the front entrance and he covered it, frowning, for there was something unnatural about the stance of the motionless man.

Jordan closed in, teeth clenched as

his eyes became accustomed to the gloom. The man seemed to be about seven feet tall. Then Jordan saw that a taut rope was suspended from a beam and tied around the man's neck, and his feet were a foot off the ground. He recognized Sheriff Holder, and horror flooded him. They had hanged the old lawman! Holder's head was to one side, his tongue protruding. His eyes were staring into hell, and he was stiff and cold to the touch. Jordan noted that the sheriff's hands were tied behind his back.

Shock ran through Jordan's veins like water down a chute. He turned instantly and headed for the street. A buzzing sounded in his ears and his mind was temporarily unhinged by the appalling sight of the sheriff. The street was deserted now — no sign of Braska and his two gun pards. Jordan went along the boardwalk, his gun hand trembling with a furious eagerness.

He reached the bank without incident and entered quickly. Deane was at his desk, going over his accounts as if nothing untoward had occurred.

'Where did Braska go?' Jordan demanded, and his voice sounded like a stranger's in his own ears.

'I told them you left by the back door and they went off in the direction of the law office,' Deane replied.

Jordan spun around and departed. He strode along the sidewalk, his heels rapping the pine boards. As he neared the law office the door opened and a man appeared, sunlight glinting on a law badge pinned to his shirt. He heard Jordan's approach and swung to face him, and then bent the elbow of his right arm and reached for his holstered pistol. Jordan drew and fired. The man fell back against the door and then pitched across the doorstep. He lay on his back and his discarded gun thumped on the threshold.

Teeth clenched, Jordan lunged into the office, stepping over the wounded man. He caught a movement over by the desk and his gun swept up, covering the figure standing there. It was Braska, frozen in shock.

'Work your gun,' Jordan rasped, sliding his pistol back into its holster. 'You get an even break, Braska, and then you're dead.'

'You shoot me and you'll make yourself an outlaw,' Braska replied. 'I'm a legal deputy. Holder pinned this badge on my chest.'

'You're a liar. You're Fletch Sherwin, a bank robber, and you've got a price on your head.' Jordan lifted his left hand and pushed aside his leather vest to reveal the star Holder had given him. 'There are witnesses to swear the sheriff gave me this badge. If you're not going to draw your hogleg then I'll arrest you for the sheriff's murder, and I'll see you hang. What's it to be?'

'The sheriff's murder?' Braska frowned. 'What are you giving me? I told Holder to leave town and keep riding. He saddled up and rode out. If he's dead then I don't know a thing about it.'

'He's hanging from a beam in the

livery barn.' Jordan felt sweat break out on his forehead.

'Mebbe he hanged hisself,' Braska suggested.

'With his hands tied behind his back?'

Jordan noticed the door between the office and the cells opening slowly and flexed the fingers of his right hand. The door was suddenly jerked open and a man stepped into the doorway, levelling a pistol. Jordan reached for his gun and it came out of its holster flaming and bucking. His shot smacked into the man's chest, spinning him half-around before dumping him on the floor. He turned the weapon on Braska, who had decided to pull his Colt.

Braska looked desperate. His face was ashen, his eyes wide, and the expression on his face indicated that he knew he was beaten before he started. His gun cleared leather and was lifting to fire when Jordan triggered another shot. The bullet took Braska high in the right shoulder and he dropped his gun without firing it. He took a step forward and then twisted and fell across the desk before pitching to the floor.

Jordan restrained his breathing against the stench of burned powder but it rasped in his chest and he heaved a sigh. His ears were protesting at the shooting, which was greatly magnified by the close confines of the office. He reloaded his pistol, then holstered the deadly weapon and checked the two gunnies. Both men were dead. He removed their guns and went to Braska's side.

Braska was unconscious — blood spreading through the thin fabric on the right shoulder of his shirt. Jordan nodded. Braska would live to face a hanging. He went to the door of the office and dragged the body of the gunman on the threshold out to the sidewalk. He looked around the street and saw men emerging from buildings and moving towards him.

Henry Forder, the town mayor, was the first to reach Jordan. His face was pale but he seemed resolute.

'There were three of them,' he said in a hoarse voice.

'I got three of them,' Jordan replied. 'Two are dead, but I saved Braska for the hangman. Get the doctor over here or he might cheat us yet. We're gonna make sure now that Farron doesn't send any more gunnies in here.'

Forder turned and called to one of the approaching townsmen, who hurried off across the street.

'They ran Sheriff Holder out of town,' Forder said heavily.

'Not true. They strung the sheriff up in the livery barn. Where's my family?'

'I saw them coming into town earlier. Braska had taken over here then — him and the two gunnies. Two cowpokes with Hester were both shot down, and the gunnies drove the buckboard with your folks in it out of town, heading south.'

Jordan went back into the office. He bent over Braska, grasped him by the shoulders, and shook him.

'Come on, Braska, wake up.'

The gunman groaned but did not open his eyes. Footsteps sounded on the sidewalk and then the doorway was darkened by a shadow. Jordan turned to see a tall, slim man carrying a medical bag looking into the office. He pointed to Braska.

'I think he'll live, Doc,' he said. 'Patch him up. I need to talk to him.'

Doc Merrill went to Braska's side and made a preliminary examination. When he looked up at the watching Jordan he shook his head.

'I'll have to get him over to my office to work on him,' he said. 'You're gonna have to wait some time before he'll be in a position to talk. I reckon he'll be out for several hours.'

Jordan heaved a sigh and turned to the attendant Forder.

'I need a couple of reliable men to take care of the town while I hunt for my family,' he said. 'Anyone turning up who works for Farron gets arrested — no questions asked.'

'We can take care of that,' Forder

said. 'I'll get a couple of men in here and stay with them. It's about time we did something about Farron.'

'It's past time, I'd say. But Farron might not be a problem right now. I put a slug in him earlier this morning at his place and he could be dead. You can expect some of his crew to ride in with him, dead or alive. If he is alive then jail him, whatever his condition.'

Forder nodded, went to a gun rack and armed himself with a Greener 12-gauge double-barrelled shotgun and a box of shells.

'You said you saw Braska and his pards take my family out of town,' Jordan mused. 'How long were they gone? And did they come back with the buckboard?'

'They were away nearly an hour, and didn't bring the buckboard back with them.' Forder moved away. 'I'll get two men in here right away.'

Jordan returned to Merrill's side. The doctor was plugging the bullet wound in Braska's shoulder. The bleeding had stopped. Braska's eyelids were flickering but he was not conscious.

'Did you attend Charlie Pierce and Tom Baldwin after Braska shot them?' Jordan asked.

'I was in my office when I heard the shots. I went out immediately and found Pierce and Baldwin lying dead in the street. Braska was standing over them. He told me they had resisted arrest. He was wearing a law badge so I assumed he was telling the truth. He took the buckboard out of town, and came back alone an hour later.'

'When you've finished with Braska you can stick him in a cell. I want to find him here when I get back.'

'He won't be going anywhere for a week, I'd say.' The doctor nodded. 'He'll be in a cell when you get back.'

Jordan went out to the street. Forder was returning, accompanied by two men who were armed with rifles. Jordan was waiting for them to reach him when he heard the grating wheels of a vehicle approaching from the north. He swung around, and drew his pistol when he saw a buckboard coming along the street. Two men were sitting on the buckboard seat and two saddle-horses were tethered at the rear of the vehicle. The buckboard pulled up in front of the law office.

'I want to report a shooting that took place out at Rafter F this morning,' one of the men said, jumping down from the buckboard. He stared at the star on Jordan's shirt front and looked at the levelled gun in Jordan's hand. 'What's going on?' he demanded. 'Where's Braska? He's supposed to be running the town now.'

'Braska's in the office.' Jordan smiled. 'You men ride for Rafter F?'

'Sure as hell,' growled the man confronting him.

'Then you're both under arrest. Get rid of your guns and step into the office.'

'We got Sam Tate, the foreman, in the buckboard,' the other man protested. 'He's near dead. Several of the crew are dead. We were shot to hell this morning.'

'The doctor is in the office, tending to Braska,' Jordan said. 'Take Tate inside, but get rid of your guns pronto.'

Forder arrived at that moment and took over. Jordan stood by with his Colt in his hand until the two Rafter F men were disarmed. Tate was carried into the office and laid on a bunk in a cell. The men were locked in a cell and Jordan confronted them.

'Where's Farron?' he demanded. 'Was he hurt in the shooting?'

'Right arm busted, that's all. He's gathering men to fight back.'

Jordan was impatient now to find his family. He took his leave quickly, swung into his saddle, and rode south out of town, his keen eyes studying the tracks left by the Jordan buckboard. He had been forced to let his family out of his sight, and wanted them back before he went up against Abel Farron in a final showdown.

7

By the time he had cleared town, Jordan was filled with anxiety for his family. He pushed his horse into a mile-eating run and followed the tracks showing plainly in the dust, aware that Braska could not have taken the buckboard far if he had returned to town within the hour. But he had no idea what orders Farron had given to Braska, and there was a gnawing doubt in his mind as he looked for the vehicle.

He realized that he had made a mistake in not ensuring that he had killed Farron when he had the chance, and now the crooked rancher was gathering men to fight back. Jordan pushed on, and three miles along the trail he topped a rise and paused to survey the range ahead. An undulating landscape confronted him, raked by gullies and broken ground. He spotted a horse standing motionless two hundred yards ahead and spurred his mount forward.

As he reached the horse he saw deep wheel-tracks in the dust and horror stabbed through him when he realized that the tracks veered suddenly and disappeared into a wide gully, The horse was wearing a harness — was not a saddle-horse — and it was bloodstained.

Jordan rode to the gully and peered into it. The buckboard was below, overturned, and the second horse of the team lay motionless beneath splintered woodwork. Narrowing his eyes, Jordan was filled with disbelief as he looked around for his family. He saw a crumpled figure lying halfway down the slope of the gully and recognized Lance. He dismounted and scrambled down the slope. When he reached Lance he was relieved to find his brother alive but unconscious.

Moving down to the wreckage of the buckboard, Jordan spotted Hester lying in a depression under the vehicle. His sister called weakly as she caught his movement, and Jordan dropped to his knees and crawled under the wreckage to her side. Hester had bloodstains on her dress and there was a big discoloured bruise on her forehead.

'Travis,' she cried 'Where's Dad? I've been calling him and Lance. Are they all right?'

Jordan saw that by falling into the depression under the buckboard, Hester had escaped serious injury. The girl was badly shocked but did not seem too badly hurt. He crawled out from under the buckboard and looked around for his father, discovering him lying on his back on the other side of the gully. Saul Jordan was unconscious. He had a bruise on his right temple and his right arm was bent at an unnatural angle.

Numb with horror, Jordan searched the wreckage of the buckboard, found a coiled rope, and tied one end to the buckboard before fastening the other to the harness on the surviving horse.

Leading the horse away from the gully, the rope tautened and the buckboard was pulled upright back on to its wheels. Jordan ran down into the gully and picked up Hester. He carried her to the top of the gully, and then fetched his father and brother to her side.

Hester sat up shakily. She held a hand to her head and closed her eyes. Jordan examined his father. Saul had a broken right arm. He was deeply unconscious but breathing steadily. Lance came to his senses as Jordan bent over him. He groaned, moved his head slightly, and then opened his eyes.

'Travis!' he exclaimed. 'What happened?'

'I was about to ask Hester,' Jordan replied.

'We got to town safely, and that's when our troubles started,' Hester said. 'Braska was there with two gunnies. He attacked Charlie and Tom — shot them down in the street when they tried to resist. Then they made us drive out of town, and when we got here they spooked the horses and ran the wagon into the gully at speed. I thought we were going to die. It was a wicked thing they did. You'll have to do something about Braska, Travis.'

'I've already done it.' Jordan explained the incidents that had occurred in town, his voice tight with suppressed fury. 'I'm gonna have to leave you out here while I fetch help. I'll go back to town for the doctor and bring another buckboard out. Will you be all right until I get back? I don't think anything could happen now. I'll be gone about an hour.'

'Just give me a pistol and I'll watch out for trouble,' Lance said tensely.

Jordan took his leave and rode back to Oak Bend. He sent Doc Merrill out to the gully and then went into the livery barn. A youth promised to take a buckboard out to the gully as soon as possible, and Jordan rode along to the law office to check on the security of the town.

Henry Forder was in the office with one of the special deputies.

'No trouble around here,' the mayor reported, and gasped in horror when Jordan explained what he had found at the gully.

'I've got to go back out there,' Jordan said. 'I won't feel easy until I've got my family back in town.'

'We'll put them up in the hotel when they arrive,' Forder said. 'I've asked around town about forming a posse to go out after Farron. You can't let him run loose after these dreadful incidents. He's riding roughshod over the whole county, and must be made to pay for it.'

'His days are numbered,' Jordan responded. 'You need to appoint a new sheriff and some good deputies. Get things moving before anything else occurs. I'll be back shortly, and then I'm riding out after Farron.'

Jordan rode south again, and galloped back to the gully. He passed a buckboard being driven in the same direction and waved encouragement to the youthful driver. When he reached the gully he found Hester kneeling beside Doc Merrill, who was attending to his father. Saul was still unconscious. His arm was already bandaged and in a sling. Jordan stood by until the doctor had finished his treatment.

'I don't like this coma Saul is in,' Merrill remarked. 'He was still suffering the after-effects of the bullet wound in the head, and now he's been knocked unconscious. There's no telling what effect it will have on him. Is a buckboard on the way?'

'It'll be here in about twenty minutes,' Jordan replied.

'Good. The sooner we get Saul into a bed and resting comfortably the better.'

Jordan paced up and down, such was his impatience. Merrill left to return to town. The buckboard arrived and Saul was lifted into it. Hester sat beside her father and Lance hunched in a corner of the vehicle. Jordan tied the surviving harness-horse to the back of the buckboard and rode to one side as the vehicle returned to Oak Bend. He was badly shaken by what had happened and had to struggle to remain calm while his every instinct urged him to take drastic action against Abel Farron.

He was greatly relieved when they reached town. They stopped at the doctor's house and Merrill emerged to take charge of Saul, who was carried inside for more treatment. Merrill insisted on keeping Saul in his charge, vowing that the rancher would be safe in his hands. Jordan took Hester and Lance to the hotel, and Hester broke down and cried when she was settled into a room. Lance entered the room next door and sat on the foot of bed clutching a .45, gazing vacantly into space.

Jordan went along to the law office, eager now to get on with his job. Henry Forder and two deputies were in the office.

'First, I got to tell you that Sam Tate died while the doc was working on him,' Forder said. 'Merrill didn't hold out much hope for him. Everyone around town is asking who shot him and wounded Farron. The two prisoners, who brought in Tate from Rafter F, said an unknown rider showed up at their ranch and started shooting without warning. Would you know anything about that, Travis?'

'Sure. I did it. I'll make a full report about what's happened when I can get round to it. I had proof that Farron was causing trouble for my family, so I hit him where it hurt most.'

'I ain't complaining,' Forder said quickly. 'Everyone knows what Farron is. It's a great pity you didn't kill him when you had your gun on him.'

'His time will come,' Jordan said grimly.

'All the able-bodied men in town are prepared to ride as possemen if you will lead them,' Forder continued. 'There's a new attitude coming out of the bad things that have been done. Folk ain't happy about the way Sheriff Holder was strung up in the livery barn. Oak Bend will no longer stand by and let the bad men run roughshod over the community. We'll hold an election for a new sheriff as soon as possible, and the council want you to act in that capacity until we have another man in office.'

'I'll do that,' Jordan agreed. 'I want a dozen possemen to ride out to Rafter F as soon as possible. With Farron and the rest of his crew behind bars, there'll be no more trouble around here.'

'As far as I know, Farron was operating with a couple of the other local ranchers — Two-Finger Dack and Pete Hillyard. Leastways, that's the way the talk has been going. They're both reckoned to throw a wide loop, although it ain't been proved. I've talked to the two men who brought in Sam Tate. They won't admit to anything, but they did say Farron rode out from his spread with half a dozen men to round up support before making a drive to nail you. I hope you've got him on the run, but I think he's too set in his ways to give up without a fight.'

'I'll make a clean sweep across the

range when I get started,' Jordan promised. 'I need to hire a new outfit for Box J when I can get around to it'

'I can't advise you on that.' Forder shook his head. 'It's impossible to know who is honest around here.'

'I'm gonna talk to Jingle Bob. He might have some ideas.'

'Doc Merrill has got him at his place. From what Doc said earlier, Jingle Bob ain't too badly hurt.'

'I want to employ a couple of men to watch my family,' Jordan mused. 'I won't feel easy riding out of town on law work and leaving my kin unprotected.'

'I'll arrange cover for them, if they stick around town.' Forder offered. 'You go ahead with the cleanup, Travis, and I'll ramrod the town until you get back. I'll have a posse ready to ride by the time you want to leave. You better take a dozen men with you. One good battle with Farron should end his crooked reign around here.'

Jordan felt easier in his mind when he left the office to walk to the doctor's house. Oak Bend was quiet, and there seemed to be a different atmosphere about the little township. Doc Merrill opened the door to him.

'No change in your father's condition,' Merrill reported.

'I know he's in good hands,' Jordan replied. 'I've come to talk to Jingle Bob. I have to leave town shortly, and I want to do something about hiring a new outfit for Box J.'

'Jingle Bob is gonna be all right. He'll be confined to a bed for several days, but he should be up and walking by the end of the week. He won't be able to sit a horse for a couple of weeks, but there's no reason why he can't get back to business.'

Jordan was eager to talk to the Box J foreman, and the doctor showed him into a back bedroom in the big house. Jones was propped up in a bed, his face pale and his eyes showing shock, but he brightened visibly when he saw Jordan.

'What's goin' on, Travis?' he demanded.

'I heard some shooting, and Doc says Charlie and Tom were killed out there on the street. Gimme a couple of days, and when I'm able to hold a gun we'll get started on Farron.'

'You don't need to worry about a thing, Jingle Bob,' Jordan replied. 'It's all under control. The ranch is left without a crew at the moment, so if you've got any ideas where we can get some reliable men then I'll be glad to hear them.'

'We don't have any work for an outfit.' Jones shook his head. 'Farron ain't left us enough stock to shake a stick at. What's the use of a crew if they ain't got cattle to work?'

'We'll buy fresh stock. I've got a pile of dough stashed in my bank account When you're on your feet we'll buy several thousand head and start up the ranch again.'

'You'll need a good crew.' Jones shook his head again. 'But I think you'll be throwing away good money if you restock now.'

'Farron ain't got long to go.' Jordan spoke confidently. 'I'm taking out a posse to hunt him down. I've already broken the back of his gang. The law is strong in town again, and there are enough men available for a posse that will keep the crooked element on the run.'

'It sounds all right. But Farron won't quit.'

'Who says he's gonna get the chance to?' Jordan smiled. 'If he doesn't get killed then he'll surely hang for what he's done. He's the big boss of the crooked bunch operating around here, and his chickens will soon be coming home to roost.'

'You've got Two-Finger Dack and Pete Hillyard to deal with, and God knows how many more rustling gangs are working the range from the canyon country. I reckon there are more rustlers than cattle in this neck of the woods, and talking of the canyon country, I got a feeling most of the rustled steers are still being held over there.'

'I'll check it out after I've nailed Farron. Now tell me where I can get some good men.'

'I wish I could. You better wait till I'm on my feet again and then I'll put out the word that we're hiring.'

'OK. You lie there and get better and then we'll set to work.'

Jordan left the doctor's house and went along to the general store. He saw riders moving along the street. Men were assembling outside the jail, and saddle-horses stood hip-shot in the sun. There were men in the store getting ammunition for their weapons, and Jordan stocked up on shells for his rifle and pistol. Most of the men he saw were strangers, but there were some faces he remembered from his past, and most of them regarded him with curiosity. His actions had been well discussed.

A dozen men were ready to ride with him when he returned to the law office. He told them what he intended doing and outlined how it should be done, and there was a chorus of assent from the possemen. They rode out fast and headed for Rafter F.

Several of the men he knew from way back rode up beside Jordan and had a few words with him. All expressed their desire to see an end to the trouble, and they were prepared to fight for what they believed in. When they breasted a rise and saw Rafter F before them, sprawled around Sweetwater Creek, Jordan called a halt and they studied the silent ranch.

'It's deserted,' someone remarked. 'We're too late, it looks like.'

'Six of you ride round to the left and get behind the spread before the rest of us move in,' Jordan directed. 'I want to arrest anyone who is here. Give them a chance to surrender, but don't let anyone get away.'

Half the posse turned aside and began to circle the ranch, keeping out of sight. Jordan watched their progress, and when they were in position he led the remainder of his law party down the slope and into Farron's yard.

They didn't need to search the spread to know that it was deserted, but possemen with drawn guns closed in and went through the silent buildings, coming back to Jordan to report no signs of the crew.

'Take a look around the yard for tracks,' Jordan said. 'If Farron left with half a dozen riders then they should be easy to follow.'

Fresh tracks were discovered heading out of the yard to the north-west, and Jordan led the posse in the same direction. He knew the range intimately, and was aware that there were vast canyons in the rough country into which they were heading where thousands of cattle could be held indefinitely. They rode at a steady pace, alert and ready for action.

Late afternoon found them in the high country. Progress became more difficult but they continued, for the tracks they were following were plain to see and they were all keen to force a showdown with Farron. Night came swiftly and they camped in a gully. Dawn found them saddling up, and after a skimpy breakfast they continued.

The desolate country unfolded as they rode on, and still the tracks beckoned them, heading deeper into the wilderness. Jordan noticed that the fresh tracks were following a well-defined trail that had been made by the passage of many cattle over a long period of time. The rustlers had not taken the trouble to blot the trail, probably because they held the initiative in this territory. The law had never pursued them and they had just grown careless. The posse rode silently, determined to bring the fleeing rustlers to account.

The sun was high overhead when one of the possemen, scouting ahead, appeared on a rise and waved excitedly. They closed in and dismounted in cover.

'There's a canyon just ahead,' the scout said, grinning broadly. 'We found the rustlers, and most of the cattle they've stolen over the past year, I should think.'

Jordan rode on with the scout and veered left when they reached a narrow defile that led into the canyon.

'I saw movement in that opening,' the scout said, 'so I guess Farron has got a man on guard. If we go this way we won't be seen. We can leave our horses in cover and climb up to the rim of the canyon.'

A faint game trail gave access up the rocky wall that blocked their way. Jordan told the possemen to rest until he returned and checked his pistol before following the scout. They ascended the bluff to a rock-strewn, wind-swept wilderness that opened out to even higher ground which was bleak and rocky. The scout edged to his right and Jordan followed until they reached the canyon rim.

Looking over the rim, Jordan found the change in scenery breathtaking. The canyon was two miles wide and curved away into the illimitable distance, startlingly green with an unbroken carpet of lush grass. A stream meandered through its centre, glinting in the sunlight, and hundreds of steers were grazing across what was a veritable oasis.

'Will you look at that?' The scout's eyes glinted at the sight of the cattle. 'There's a hut down there in the trees, and a corral with half a dozen horses in it.'

'I see them.' Jordan nodded. 'Let's get down and ride in on them. I'll be interested to see what brands are on those steers.'

They returned to the posse, saddled up and rode to the canyon entrance. Jordan went ahead, gun in hand, but saw no signs of guards. He reined up on the threshold of the grass to wait for the posse to join him.

'Some of you sneak around to the far side of the hut,' he directed. 'Stick close to the wall of the canyon and you should make it without being seen. I'll ride in from this side and we'll have them cold.'

The possemen were eager to fight, and Jordan dismounted with half the men and they waited while the rest sneaked away, leading their horses. They disappeared in thick undergrowth and tense minutes flitted by. Silence hung like a blanket over them. Jordan could not relax. He held his rifle ready for action and his gaze probed and searched the area for signs of the rustlers.

'I spotted one of our men behind the shack,' a posseman reported. 'It was Dick Lintock, and he waved his rifle. I guess they're ready for us to move in.'

Jordan nodded and they mounted and rode into the canyon. The shack was partially obscured by the trees surrounding it, but the rustlers would have a man on watch, just in case. They rode at a canter, guns ready, in line abreast, and eagerness was bubbling in Jordan's chest. He wanted to put an end to Abel Farron, and if the Rafter F rancher was here in the canyon then his rustling days were over.

The sound of their hoofs thudded in the lush grass, and yard by yard they advanced to the gurgling stream where the shack was situated. They were within fifty yards of the little building when a man stepped out of cover. He was holding a rifle and stood eyeing them as they approached.

Jordan was holding his pistol in his right hand, and covered the man from the moment he saw him. The guard suddenly decided that the newcomers were hostile and lifted his rifle to his shoulder. Jordan fired instantly, and as the crash of the shot rang out the guard twisted and fell into a heap. Harsh echoes fled across the canyon and reverberated.

'Let's get in there,' Jordan called, and spurred his horse forward.

The possemen followed closely, but before they reached the shack by the water's edge a fusillade of shots blasted, shattering the stillness. Jordan. hunched low in his saddle and drove his horse on. The shooting increased rapidly, and suddenly figures were emerging hurriedly from the shack, and the men backing Jordan joined in the shooting . . .

8

The men fleeing from the shack ran desperately towards the corral. Jordan started shooting, his eyes narrowed against the shadows under the trees. Five men had appeared, and they were intent on shooting it out with the possemen Jordan had sent around the shack to cut off escape to the rear. Jordan's first shot sent a rustler sprawling into the undergrowth, and made the rustlers aware that they were surrounded. The corral was out in the open and the rustlers dropped in cover just short of their horses. The posse men poured a hot fire into the area.

Jordan called for a ceasefire and the shooting dwindled away. When silence came, Jordan arose to one knee and addressed the rustlers.

'This is a posse from Oak Bend,' he shouted. 'You are surrounded so throw down your guns and come out with your hands up. This is the only chance you'll get. If you fight on we'll wipe you out.'

A rustler fired a shot that clipped Jordan's hat brim and shooting was resumed. The posse began to close in. One by one the rustlers were shot down, until the remaining two made a desperate dash for the corral and their horses. Guns blasted and they dropped in their tracks. The echoes faded and the possemen closed in with ready guns.

The possemen were exultant as they dragged the rustlers together in front of the corral. There were eight altogether, and six were dead. Jordan examined the two survivors. One was dying — the other was not so seriously wounded. The possemen searched the area for Abel Farron but there was no sign of the crooked rancher.

'Farron rides a grey horse,' one of the possemen said. 'I don't see it here. It looks like he's got away. He's smart enough to send his men here while he rode off somewhere else.'

'See what you can do for the wounded man,' Jordan directed. 'I want to take a look at the cattle.'

He mounted and rode on into the canyon. Cattle were grazing on the far side of the stream, and he was pleased to see that the majority were branded Box J. He returned to the shack to find the wounded man conscious and being prepared for the trip back to town.

Jordan questioned the rustler but the man was not inclined to talk.

'Does anyone know any of these men?' Jordan asked the possemen.

'Most of them rode for Farron,' someone replied.

'This one didn't,' another said, indicating one of the dead rustlers. 'I've seen him in town with Two-Finger Dack.'

'I've heard that Dack and Hillyard are rustling along with Farron,' Jordan mused.

'There could be some truth in that,'

was the general opinion. 'Dack swings a wide loop, and Pete Hillyard would go along with anything Dack suggests. The two of them have been pretty thick with Farron.'

'So Farron would most likely go to either of their ranches to look for more help.' Jordan nodded. 'OK. Let's head back to town. I'm gonna have to get another crew for Box J, and the first job they'll do is fetch this herd back to where it belongs.'

They rode out, taking the wounded rustler with them, and headed back towards Oak Bend. Jordan had plenty to think about as they travelled, and when he found the wounded man slowing their progress he directed two of the possemen to bring him along at a more leisurely pace while the posse pushed on.

Night found them still many miles from town and they camped for a few hours. They were ready to ride when the sun came up next morning, and Jordan had decided to change his plans.

The possemen were tired and silent, and he doubted if they would want to do anything but ride straight back to town.

'I need to get Farron as soon as possible,' he said. 'He won't be sitting around town waiting for us to ride in and take him, so I think we should keep looking for him until we get him. We could angle east from here and take a look around Dack's spread. With any luck we just might drop on to Farron, and that will end the trouble.'

There were protests from some of the men.

'Some of us have a business to run,' one said.

'We all got jobs,' another put in. 'We've given the law a good run. It's time to get back to town.'

'Then I'll cut off on my own,' Jordan decided. 'You men can go back to town. Put the prisoner behind bars. I'll swing around by Dack's place, and if Farron ain't there I'll take a look over Hillyard's spread. I want Farron.'

Taking his leave of the posse, he rode north-east. It had been many years since he had travelled in this direction, but he knew the range intimately and arrived in view of Dack's Flying D just before sundown. He stepped down from his saddle in cover and stretched to get the kinks out of his powerful figure as he studied the ranch. The sun was going down in a blaze of red and gold behind his back and the last light of the passing day threw the buildings of the ranch into bold relief.

Two men were on the porch of the house and Jordan used his field glasses to check for Farron. He knew Dack by sight, and recognized him sitting in a rocker in the shade. The other man was pacing to and fro on the boards; a stranger to Jordan. Dressed in a store-suit, he was obviously not a ranch hand. Jordan directed his glasses to the bunkhouse off to the left, saw no movement, and studied the cook-shack, which looked strangely deserted — no smoke was issuing from its chimney.

Jordan sat back on his heels. Apart from Dack and the stranger, the ranch was devoid of life at the busiest time of day. The crew would normally be eating now, and Jordan wondered if Farron had taken them in an attempt to regain the initiative. He began to fear that if he had got the rights of it then Farron might now be in Oak Bend, where the Jordan family was practically defence-less.

There was only one way to get at the true situation. Jordan paused only to remove the deputy star from his shirt front, and then swung into his saddle and rode out into the open. He headed into the ranch, alert for trouble, and rode to the house, aware that he was under close scrutiny from the moment he left cover.

Two-Finger Dack did not move from his seat, but Jordan saw the rancher pick up a Winchester that had been leaning against the side of his rocking chair. The rancher held the rifle across his knees. As he reined up in front of the porch, Jordan could see that Dack was missing the first two fingers of his left hand — lost in the civil war. The rancher was looking sickly. His thin face was angular, dark eyes sunken, cheeks hollow. He looked like a man who had swallowed bad water.

'Who in hell are you?' Dack rasped.

'I'm looking for Abel Farron,' Jordan sat with his hands on his saddlehorn. 'I stopped off at Rafter F but he'd left, and I heard he'd come on here.'

'What do you want with him?' Dack demanded.

'A riding job. Friend of mine said Farron was hiring good men, but it seems the thing to do is find him.'

'What friend was that?' Dack moved impatiently.

The other man on the porch had ceased his pacing as Jordan reined in, and stood motionless, his narrowed eyes studying Jordan impassively.

'Frank Lyle,' Jordan said.

'Lyle is dead! Some gunnie working for Box J killed him.' Dack straightened in his chair and took a fresh grip on his rifle, lifting the muzzle slightly to cover Jordan. 'Farron told me about it when he was here around noon. He went on to Oak Bend with my crew.'

'I heard about it at Rafter F when I stopped by. I rode back to town and killed the man who shot Lyle. Farron's had his ride for nothing. I've saved him the job. I reckoned he'd take me on when he knew what I'd done.'

'Well, Farron ain't here. You've had your ride for nothing.'

'Is he coming back here?' Jordan persisted.

'He didn't say. He's got a lot of trouble on his plate right now and he's like a cat on hot bricks — there's no telling which way he'll jump next. If you want some grub then go over to the cook-shack and help yourself. Farron even took my cook with him today.'

'Thanks, but I'd better head back to town if that's where Farron is.'

'And when you see him, tell him to

send my crew back, and warn him Deke Moran is here waiting to do business for the herd that's ready for sale.' Dack set his rifle down beside the chair. 'I need my damn crew. The work around here won't get done by itself.'

The rancher pushed himself to his feet and went into the house, followed by Moran. Jordan turned away and rode back across the yard, experiencing a tingling sensation between his shoulder blades until he regained cover beyond the gate. Shadows were dense now. He gazed back at the ranch. Dack had lit a lamp in the big living-room and a yellow glare stained the front windows of the house.

So Farron was ready to sell cattle, Jordan mused, and thought of the big Box J herd in the canyon that had been rustled. He needed to forestall that deal, he decided, and dismounted to tie his horse to a branch in the brush. He stood for a moment, his thoughts flitting over the situation, and then sighed and walked back to Dack's ranch house. If he took Moran into custody on suspicion of intending to buy stolen stock then there would be no danger of the herd in the canyon getting into the wrong hands.

He stepped carefully on to the porch and peered through the lighted window. Dack and Moran were in the big living-room, seated in leather chairs and holding glasses of whiskey. Moran was talking in a high-pitched complaining tone. Jordan drew his pistol and threw open the front door. He strode into the house and covered the two men. Both froze at his entrance.

'I don't like the thought of Moran waiting out here for Farron,' Jordan said, 'so I think he'd better ride into town with me.'

'What the hell!' Dack ejaculated. 'Moran is my guest. He'll wait here until Farron gets back.'

'I'm not asking him to go with me, I'm telling him.' Jordan waggled his pistol. 'If you wanta argue then I'll take you too, Dack.'

'I ain't well enough to go anywhere,' Dack replied.

'Then shut up and sit still,' Jordan warned. 'You got a horse around here, Moran?'

'In the barn,' Moran said.

'We'll fetch it, but first you better get rid of any hardware you got on you.'

Moran was not wearing a gunbelt. He reached into an inside pocket in his jacket, produced a short-barrelled pistol, and dropped it to the floor.

'Now get that rope off the wall and hogtie Dack. Then we'll head out.'

Moran obeyed, and Jordan tested the knots on Dack before he was satisfied. He picked up a lamp and conducted Moran to the barn. The cattle-buyer saddled up and they walked across the yard to where Jordan's horse was tethered. Jordan mounted and they set out for Oak Bend.

The long ride to town was silent. Moran made no attempt to resist or escape. Jordan was alert, listening for unnatural sounds and watching the shadows for trouble. He was tired but resolute, and it was after midnight when he spotted the distant lights of Oak Bend. They entered the silent town and reined in at the law office.

'Are you some kind of a lawman?' Moran demanded as they dismounted.

'Deputy Sheriff.' Jordan drew his gun and covered the cattle-buyer. 'We'll talk about the cattle deal you're hoping to pull off. If it's for the herd I think it is then you're in a lot of trouble, Moran.'

'I don't know anything about local problems,' Moran replied. 'Farron is a rancher, and if he's got cattle for sale then I'm ready to buy them. That ain't against the law. I've been in the business for twenty years.'

Jordan ushered Moran into the office. Henry Forder was seated at the desk. His face was badly bruised. He got quickly to his feet when he saw Jordan.

'Am I glad to see you, Travis,' he said. 'The posse got back earlier, and from what they said, your trip was successful. We had some trouble here this afternoon when Farron rode in with near a dozen of Dack's riders. Farron was after you. He took some convincing that you weren't around, and roughed me up. There was nothing I could do against a dozen men, and Farron took Braska out of the cells when he left. He reckoned to come back when you were here.'

'What about my family?' Jordan demanded.

'Farron knew they weren't at Box J, and sent two men to the hotel. They took Hester when the bunch rode out. Farron wanted to take Saul as well, but Doc Merrill told them that moving your dad might kill him so he was left. I spoke to Lance afterwards, and he said they told Hester that you had been shot bad out of town and was asking for her, but I reckon Farron took her as a hostage. I'm sorry, Travis. I did my best, but there was just too many of them for me to do anything.'

'Have you any idea where Farron

went when he left with Hester?' Jordan asked.

'No. He was close-mouthed about that.'

'He didn't ride back to Dack's place,' Jordan mused, 'so he must have returned to Rafter F. I'll ride back out there and look around. He glanced at the silent Moran. 'This is Deke Moran, a cattle-buyer come to take a herd off Farron's hands. Lock him up and keep him safe until I get back. I reckon he's after the herd we found in the canyon. I should be back tomorrow morning, if I can get a fresh horse from the stable.'

'Take mine,' Forder said. 'It's in the stable. Tell Seth I said you can use it.'

Jordan saw Moran into a cell and then departed quickly. He paused in the open doorway of the hotel, decided to see his brother Lance, and entered quietly. Lance was asleep in his room, and Jordan shook him awake.

'Travis, I've been hoping you'd hurry back. The posse got in hours ago. I wanted to go out after Farron but I ain't in a fit state to fight him and his bunch.'

'I'm glad you stuck around here,' Jordan told him. 'Is Dad safe?'

'Sure. Farron heard he was with the doc but Merrill said he couldn't be moved, and Farron took Hester instead. He didn't bother about me, beyond telling me what would likely happen to Hester if I didn't sit tight here in town. Can I ride with you, Travis?'

'No. Stay here and keep an eye on Dad. I'll go after Farron alone. I've got a big score to settle with him and I don't want anyone getting in my way.'

'Sure. But you take it easy out there, Travis. Farron was in a real bad mood. He had an arm in a sling but that wasn't stopping him.'

'It's a pity I didn't kill him when I had the chance,' Jordan replied. 'I won't make any mistake the next time I get him in my sights.'

He departed, picked up Forder's horse from the stable and left town. The night was still and silent and he rode steadily towards Rafter F, his thoughts moving at the speed of light although he knew what he had to do. If he put Farron out of business then all the trouble would cease. He knew the kind of men riding for Farron. They were a breed peculiar to the wilderness — vicious wolves of the range that cared only about the money in their pockets and had no qualms of conscience how they had to earn it. Life was cheap to them, and they were not guided by the laws governing honest folk. Jordan had no compunction in shooting them down like dogs.

Dawn was beginning to lighten the night sky when Jordan reined up on a knoll and looked across Sweetwater Creek at the grey huddle of buildings that was the Rafter F ranch headquarters. There were no lights about the place, but he did not doubt that guards were in position, covering the approaches. He left his mount in cover, took his rifle, and moved in on foot, easing forward from cover to cover; watching his surroundings and listening for unnatural noise.

He had to get Hester away from Farron before he could even think about attacking this crooked bunch. Once his sister was safe he could wade into these men and ram justice down their throats. He circled the yard, passing between the bunkhouse and the barn, and stood in the shadows surrounding the cook-shack for some minutes. He could just see that there were horses in the corral but he had not seen a guard yet, and that bothered him. Farron would not take any risks at this stage of the fight.

He was about to move on when he caught a faint smell of cigarette smoke and turned his head slowly until he was looking directly into the breeze. A clump of cottonwoods on the bank of the stream held dark shadows, and he saw a faint red glow brighten and then fade as someone drew on a cigarette.

Jordan moved slowly then, stalking the man, and tense minutes passed as he crossed open ground. He could hear the bubbling and gurgling of the stream in the background. A man coughed. Jordan reached a cottonwood and straightened. He drew his pistol and peered around the tree. Dawn was breaking now and his eyes were able to pick out details of the objects around him.

The guard was sitting on a rock with his back to the stream. His rifle was lying across his knees, the muzzle pointing away from Jordan. Jordan cocked his pistol. The three clicks sounded loud and the guard's head jerked up as he came to full alertness. He began to lift his rifle.

'Drop the gun,' Jordan rapped. 'And sit still or you're dead.'

The man froze instantly, and a moment later his rifle thudded on the ground. Jordan stepped out from behind the tree and confronted him. Full daylight was creeping in, chasing away the shadows under the trees.

'Where in hell did you spring from?'

the guard demanded.

'I'll ask the questions,' Jordan rasped. 'Where's Hester Jordan?'

'Who's she?'

Jordan swung his rifle left-handed and crashed the muzzle against the side of the man's head.

'No smart talk. Just answer the questions. Where's the girl?'

'She ain't here. Farron ain't that stupid. He said you'd be around looking for her, and took her someplace safe with a couple of men to guard her.'

'Where is she?' Jordan repeated.

'Farron didn't say where they were taking her, and that's the truth.'

'Is Farron here?'

'No. There are only two of us. We're taking it in turns to guard the place.'

'You must know where Farron has gone. Tell me or take a beating.'

'I swear I don't know.'

'What direction did Farron take when he left?'

'He rode north-east.'

A faint drumming sound in the

background was growing steadily louder. Jordan struck the guard with his rifle butt. The man gasped and fell off the rock, unconscious. Jordan removed the man's pistol from its holster and stepped in behind a tree. He watched five riders entering the yard. They rode openly towards the house and reined up in front of the porch.

'Hello the house. Anyone at home?' one called.

Tense moments passed, and then a tall, thin man appeared in the doorway of the house, holding a rifle. There was a short exchange of words which Jordan could not hear, and then the riders turned and rode back the way they had come. Jordan waited until they had gone, then crossed the yard as the man on the porch withdrew inside the house again.

Jordan reached the front corner of the house and cat-footed along the side to the rear corner and edged along the back wall. He approached the kitchen window and peered through. The man who had been on the porch was now getting himself some breakfast. Jordan reached the back door. He tried the handle, found the door unlocked, and opened it to step into the kitchen, his pistol in his right hand. He closed the door at his back with a spurred heel and the slam of it brought the man swinging round.

'Who in hell are you?' the man demanded. 'Where did you come from?'

'I'm looking for Farron and a girl,' Jordan replied. 'Get rid of your gun and we'll talk.'

The man relieved himself of his Colt. His narrowed brown eyes were steady on Jordan's face.

'Don't even think about trying what's in your mind,' Jordan said.

'Farron ain't here.' The man shrugged. 'He rode on last night, leaving just two of us here.'

'Where did he go?'

'I don't know. It looked to me that he was headed for Circle H, Hillyard's place, but that ain't likely because Pete

Hillyard and some of his crew were here just now, asking after Farron. There's no one here but me and Catton.'

'Catton is asleep by the creek.' Jordan was satisfied that the man was telling the truth for his words corresponded with what the guard by the stream had said.

He walked around the man and then struck him with his pistol. The man dropped unconscious to the floor and Jordan prepared himself some breakfast. He ate quickly, wanting to be on the trail as soon as he had checked for hoofprints in the yard. He did not need anyone to tell him where Abel Farron had gone. He would follow the crooked rancher clear into hell if he had to.

9

The sun was shining by the time Jordan went out to the yard. He carried his rifle and crossed to the corral to check over countless hoofprints in the thick dust. He looked the ground over unhurriedly, and finally found four sets of tracks heading off into the north-east that had been made within the last twelve hours. He fetched his horse, attended to its needs, and then set out to follow the tracks Farron had left.

Jordan was concerned for Hester. Farron was playing a deep game, and there had to be an ulterior motive for his abduction of Hester. Jordan rode fast, for the tracks were easy to follow, and he noted that Farron had moved quickly after leaving Rafter F. Jordan knew where Hillyard's Circle H was located, and it seemed as if Farron was heading straight for it, but, three miles from Rafter F, the tracks swung abruptly and headed south.

Jordan reined in and looked around, puzzled by Farron's change of direction. He went on alertly, his hand close to the butt of his pistol. Was Farron riding back to Oak Bend? He pushed on resolutely, watching the tracks keenly. He searched his mind for what lay ahead, and the town seemed to be the only answer.

He began to get a warning in the back of his mind; an increasing awareness that he was not alone, and minutes later, as he was ascending an incline, he caught a glimpse of sunlight reflecting from metal at the top of the rise. His sharp gaze picked out the outline of a man's head and shoulders and he dived out of his saddle a split second before a rifle shot split the silence. A bullet crackled past him too close for comfort as he hit the slope hard and rolled into a slight depression.

A string of shots blasted, hurling a string of echoes through the otherwise silent morning. Jordan heard slugs striking the ground all around his position. One bullet plucked at the crown of his Stetson and he hunched lower to the ground, unable to raise his head because of the volume of fire. He had drawn his pistol the instant he hit the ground, and lay waiting for the moment when he could use it.

The shooting came from at least four weapons, he guessed, and he wondered who had ambushed him. He removed his hat and risked a glance over his cover. Gun smoke was hazing the skyline but he saw figures up there, and two of them were climbing into saddles. Jordan thrust up his pistol and triggered three shots. He saw one of the riders pitch off his horse before return fire forced his head down and he took the opportunity to reload.

Pounding hoofs warned him of more trouble and slugs began striking all around his position. Two riders at least were coming down the slope, and he clenched his teeth and waited for the right moment to confront them.

When he pushed himself above his cover the two riders were only yards from him. Jordan started shooting as the riders opened fire. A bullet burned his left arm just above the elbow and another caught the top of his left shoulder. Pain slashed through him and he ducked, but cut loose with his pistol. His first shot took the rider on the left through the centre of the chest, throwing him backwards. The man lost his balance and fell from his saddle. His left foot caught in the stirrup and his horse galloped by Jordan's position, dragging the rider.

The second man was several yards behind and his Colt blasted unceasingly, throwing lead all around Jordan, who drew a bead on the fast-moving figure and squeezed his trigger, ignoring the shooting. The rider slumped in his saddle, fell forward over the neck of his horse, and then slipped to the ground. He bounced on the slope and slithered towards Jordan, coming to rest with his head only two feet away.

Jordan ducked as more shots came at him from the crest. He kept low and reloaded the spent chambers in his pistol before rising up and snapping off three shots. One of the rifles above him stopped shooting, and then silence came and gun echoes died slowly.

'Hey, you down there. Throw out your gun and stand up. We got you pinned down. You can't get away.'

The voice was harsh and loud, and Jordan narrowed his eyes when he recognized it. Pete Hillyard. He pictured the rancher who was rumoured to be another of Farron's crooked associates.

'Come and get me, Hillyard!' he replied, and grinned when a fusillade of shots rang out. Bullets thudded around him and he kept low until the storm ceased.

'I always thought you were a no-hoper, Hillyard,' Jordan called. 'Can't you see that Farron is finished around here? I've shot the guts out of his outfit and I'm gonna take him soon as I get my sights on him. You'd be wise to get the hell out of this instead of trying to fight me.'

'Who in hell are you?' Hillyard demanded.

'I'm wearing a deputy sheriff badge, which puts you on the spot. You're fighting the law now.'

'The hell you say! If that's the truth then show yourself and let me see your badge.'

'Throw down your guns and come out into the open,' Jordan countered.

Three guns blasted in a furious racket of echoing sound and Jordan hugged the ground and waited. Pain was coursing through his left shoulder and he could feel blood trickling. He risked a quick look up the slope, saw three riders sitting on the sky line, and sent shots in their direction, but return fire made him duck before he could note the results. Sweat ran into his eyes as he reloaded his spent chambers. He risked another look and saw only two riders above.

All he was interested in was whittling down the numbers of the opposition, and in that he had been most successful. He pushed his pistol over the lip of the depression and triggered two shots at Hillyard as the crooked rancher whirled his mount and rode back into better cover. Jordan listened to the fading echoes.

There was a lull in the action, and silence pressed down on Jordan. He risked a look over his cover and a rifle threw a slug within an inch of his right ear. He ducked and waited. As far as he could tell, it was a stand-off. He could not get out of his cover and Hillyard was unable to get at him.

Minutes dragged by. Jordan began to tense for an effort that would end the impasse. He bunched his muscles to leap out of the depression and across the slope to thicker cover. In the background he heard the sudden clatter of hoofs on hard rock somewhere down the slope and alarm flared in his mind. He twisted to check his back as a rifle cracked from below.

Jordan felt a stunning blow on the right side of his head. His hat was flipped off by a bullet that came at him from an angle, and a black curtain slipped instantly over him as sight and sound fled . . .

When Jordan regained his senses he was face down across a jolting saddle and his hands were tied behind his back. His head was aching, and the wounds in his left arm and shoulder were throbbing. He opened his eyes, gazed at the ground below him, and closed them again quickly as his senses swirled. All he could hear were the creaking sounds of saddle leather and the thud of hoofs upon the hard range.

He had no idea how long he had been unconscious, and wondered where he was being taken. At least Hillyard had not shot him out of hand. He guessed he was being conveyed to wherever Abel Farron was holed up, and had no doubts about his future. Farron would shoot him without compunction. He tried without success to loosen the knotted rope around his wrists but kept drifting in and out of consciousness during the long ride. He came back to his senses as the torture of jolting along head-down across the saddle finally ended. A rough hand grasped his shoulder and he was dragged off the horse and allowed to fall heavily to the ground. He remained motionless, his senses spinning, and when he tried to open his eyes he found that the right eye was crusted with blood and he was unable to see with it.

'Come on, get up,' Hillyard rasped. 'You ain't dead yet.'

Jordan feigned unconsciousness. He heard boots thudding on the hard ground, the tinkle of spur rowels, and risked a glance around with his one good eye. He saw Hillyard stepping up on to a porch and frowned. Where was he? He twisted his head and looked around the yard of a ranch, and it filtered into his bemused mind that this was Box J.

Was Farron here? If he was then he had played a master stroke by hiding out in the one place Jordan would never have thought to look for him. And was Hester here, a prisoner in her own home? Jordan forced himself to relax. He could do nothing while his wrists were tied. He had to play this as it came. If he got a chance to gain the upper hand he had to be ready to seize it.

He breathed slowly through his gaping mouth. A horse stamped. The heat was powerful on his face. He watched the door of the house, and presently Hillyard reappeared, followed by Abel Farron. The diminutive Rafter F rancher was gaunt-faced. His left arm was in a sling. The two ranchers came off the porch and stood over Jordan, who could almost feel the intensity of their combined malevolent gazes.

'Is he dead?' Farron demanded in a scratchy tone.

'Nope. He's playing possum, I reckon.' Hillyard grasped Jordan's right shoulder and shook it roughly. 'Come on, you ain't hurt bad. Open your eyes and say howdy to the boss. You been giving him enough grief these past days, so wake up and take what's coming to you.'

Jordan groaned, but kept his eyes closed tightly and let his head roll a little.

'Bring him into the house and we'll patch him up,' Farron said. 'I can use him. The Jordan gal told me he's her brother Travis, come home to help the family. I figured him for a gunnie, but he's Travis Jordan, and now I've got him I can play a different game. I'll kill Saul Jordan, Travis will inherit this spread, and he can sign it over to me before I kill him. I've been waiting for Saul Jordan to come back to his senses to relieve him of this place, but it's looking like that will never happen.'

'Heck, you're right,' Hillyard agreed. 'It is Travis Jordan. I didn't recognize him with all that blood on him. He's been gone from this range for more than ten years. So he's the one been giving you all the trouble. If it was left to me, Abel, I'd kill him now.'

'He'll die all right, but not yet. I want to get my hands on this spread, so do like I say. Patch him up and I'll send a man into town to kill Saul Jordan.'

Hillyard and one of his two men picked up Jordan and carried him into the house. He was deposited on a leather couch and one of the gunnies was detailed to watch him. Jordan remained motionless, eyes narrowed as he watched for a chance to gain the upper hand. But it was obvious that Hillyard was taking no chances.

Farron left the room and returned minutes later with Hester. The girl uttered a cry of shock when she recognized Jordan, and ran to his side.

'He ain't hurt bad,' Hillyard rasped. 'Get some water and clean him up.'

Hester hurried out, to return moments later with a bowl of water and some cloths. She dropped to her knees beside Jordan and sponged blood from his face.

He opened his eyes, grinned up at her, and then feigned unconsciousness again. Hester checked the bullet wounds in his arm and shoulder and then bandaged them. Jordan felt better for her treatment and began to think actively about escaping.

'I'll get you some food, Travis,' Hester said, and departed for the kitchen.

Hillyard pulled Jordan into a sitting position. Farron entered the room.

'I'm going into Oak Bend,' Farron said. 'I'll take care of Saul Jordan personally, but I'll want a couple of your men along with me, Pete. I don't know what the situation is in town since Lyle was killed.'

'Heck, I only got a couple of men left,' Hillyard replied. 'Who'll stay here and watch Travis? I got to be getting back to my place.'

'You got more men at your spread so send a few over here to hold the place until I can get some of the men in from my line camps. I sent word to them, but it'll be a couple of days before they'll show up.'

'This deal is going downhill fast,' Hillyard observed. 'I'm thinking it would be better to forget the whole thing. You reckoned it would be easy to take over, but since Travis came back everything's gone wrong. You ain't got one good gunnie left standing. Even Braska is on his back.'

'We've got Travis so there's not a problem now,' Farron insisted. 'Stay here, Pete, until I get back from town.'

'All right, but I don't like it. If anything else goes wrong I'm splitting the breeze pronto. I know when to quit, if you don't.'

Farron departed, and moments later Jordan heard the sound of departing hoofs. Both Hillyard's remaining riders accompanied Farron, and Jordan began to hope that an opportunity to escape would present itself. Hillyard sat in a chair opposite, a sixgun in his hand, and his attention never wavered from his prisoner. Jordan watched Hillyard closely, urgency creeping into his mind because Farron was on his way to town to kill Saul. He tried to estimate how much time he had in which to break free and save his father.

Hester appeared after some minutes, carrying a tray on which she had placed food and two bottles of root beer. She untied Jordan's wrists and he began to eat. He was ravenous. Hester sat at his side, and Jordan tried to signal her with his eyes and expression, wanting her to create a diversion, anything that would distract Hillyard for a few vital seconds, but the Circle H rancher seemed to have a wholesome respect for Jordan and did not relax for a moment. Hester did not seem to be able to read Jordan's expression, for she gave no sign that she understood his facial signalling.

'You know you're in big trouble, Hillyard,' Jordan said at length. 'There's no way Farron can get away with this. Since I killed Frank Lyle in town the community has had a change of heart. Henry Forder took over the jail with some new deputies, and all the menfolk of the town are solidly behind the law. I took out a posse a few days ago and we discovered the cattle Farron was holding in the canyon country. I dropped in on Dack, and arrested Deke Moran, the cattle-buyer they had brought in to take those rustled steers off their hands. The bottom has fallen out of the rustling business, but Farron can't see it yet. He'll be arrested the minute he shows his face in town, and you're sitting here wasting time when you should be forking a bronc to hell and gone.'

'Save your breath,' Hillyard rasped. 'What do you take me for? You're the one in bad trouble.'

Hester left the room with the food tray. Jordan pushed himself to his feet and Hillyard lifted his gun.

'Sit still or I'll gut-shoot you,' he warned. 'You ain't got a chance. I'm in this come hell or high water, and I ain't dropping out yet.'

Jordan sat down again. Hillyard was too far away to be jumped. Hester came back and Hillyard did not even glance at her. He was watching Jordan intently. His manner was calm, resolute, but to Jordan's incisive gaze the rancher seemed ill at ease.

Hester came to Jordan's side and dropped to her knees in front of him. She examined his bandages. Her back was to Hillyard and she made a big show of tending Jordan.

'How you feeling, Travis?' she enquired.

'I'm OK. I was lucky, I guess,' he replied. 'Hillyard's men couldn't shoot straight.'

'I can,' Hillyard said. 'Just give me a chance to plug you.'

'That wouldn't suit Farron. He wants me alive to sign over this place to him,' Jordan laughed harshly. 'That won't happen in a hundred years.'

Hester got to her feet and walked to a window to gaze out across the yard. Jordan could feel tension growing inside him. He needed to be on the move. He had to stop Farron from reaching Oak Bend.

'Come away from that window, Hester,' Hillyard rapped. 'You ain't supposed to be at home.'

Hester turned to face Hillyard, and there was something in her expression that alerted Jordan. He gazed at his sister, saw her reach into a pocket of her dress, and a protest flared in his mind when she lifted her hand clear and he saw a .41 derringer gripped in her fingers. She pointed the gun at Hillyard, who was so shocked he forgot about his sixgun, and then Hester fired the small weapon.

Hillyard's face registered horror and disbelief. He thrust up his Colt as the crash of the derringer tore through the heavy silence. The bullet thumped into Hillyard's chest and he fell back in his chair, his weapon spilling from his hand. Jordan sprang up and dived across the room, his outstretched hand snatching up Hillyard's pistol, but the weapon was not needed. Hillyard was dead.

The echoes of the shot faded slowly.

Hester lowered the derringer, her face pale and resolute. Her hands trembled as she turned to Jordan.

'We'd better split the breeze to town if we're to save Dad,' she said shakily. 'Farron won't hesitate to kill him.'

'I'll go,' Jordan started for the door, checking Hillyard's gun before holstering it. 'You can follow behind if you like, but I don't want you with me when I face Farron. He won't give in without a fight.'

He left the house fast, and was swinging into his saddle when he heard the sound of horses coming into the yard. He paused, palming the pistol and cocking it. Two riders were approaching, and one of them was Braska, his right shoulder swathed in bandages, his arm in a sling. Braska was gaunt and hungover, slumped in his saddle and looking miserable. The second man was a stranger to Jordan, and he was drawing his holstered pistol.

'That's Jordan,' he yelled at Braska, levelling his pistol despite the fact that

Jordan was already covering him.

Jordan fired and the gunnie fell off his horse. Braska reached for a gun with his left hand, and then paused, the gun still in its holster. He gazed at Jordan, his expression registering hesitation.

'Get rid of it, Braska,' Jordan called. 'And be careful how you do it.'

Braska disarmed himself and sat motionless on his horse. Jordan rode in close.

'I oughta shoot you down like the dog you are,' Jordan said. 'Where have you come from?'

'Oak Bend. I'm out of this now.'

'The hell you are! You're in up to your neck.'

'I saw Farron heading for town and told him I'm quitting. I'm heading for Rafter F to pick up my gear before I make for the border, Farron asked me to drop in here to see how Hillyard is doing.'

'Hillyard's dead,' Jordan rasped. 'You'd better shake the dust of this range off your boots, because if I ever see your face again I'll put a bullet through you. Get moving, Braska, and don't stop until you hit Mexico.'

Braska shook his reins and his horse moved out. Jordan set spurs to his mount and rode on, hitting a gallop before he cleared the ranch yard. He glanced over his shoulder, saw Hester following at a distance, and faced his front to get as much speed as possible from his horse.

He was still several miles from Oak Bend when he spotted three riders ahead on the trail, and a shaft of relief stabbed through him when he recognized Farron. He hammered on, but Farron spotted him before he could get within gunshot range. The next instant the trio were pushing into a gallop, and they twisted in their saddles and cut loose with their sixguns. Gun smoke flared and echoes chased across the range.

Jordan hunched himself in his saddle and concentrated on getting more speed from his horse. He was aware that the animal was tiring and drew his

211

pistol, ignoring the shots coming at him. He fired a single shot and grinned when the right-hand rider slipped out of his saddle and hit the ground hard.

Farron reined in immediately, snatched his rifle from its saddle holster, and aimed a string of 44.40 slugs at Jordan. The first bullet struck Jordan's horse in the chest and the animal went down as if it had been pole-axed. Jordan barely had time to kick his feet out of his stirrups before the animal took a crashing fall on the hard ground. Jordan dived to his right and rolled clear, but lost his grip on his pistol. He was winded, and gasped for breath as he raised his head to stare after Farron, who galloped away over a ridge and was quickly lost to sight, followed by Hillyard's surviving rider.

Hester arrived before Jordan could attempt to get to his feet. She retrieved his pistol and stuck it in his hand as he climbed upright and stood swaying. The fall had shaken him considerably, and pain was darting through his left shoulder and arm.

'Are you all right?' Hester demanded.

'I'll do,' Jordan retorted through clenched teeth. 'Fetch that loose horse for me. I need to get on.'

Hester swung back into her saddle and went to where the horse, whose rider lay crumpled on the ground, was now grazing quietly. Jordan walked a few testing steps, found that his limbs still worked, and hurried in the same direction, checking his pistol as he did so. Hester caught the horse and came back with it, and held the reins while Jordan heaved himself into the saddle.

Jordan rode on, but had traversed only a few yards when his sense of balance lurched and he was assailed by vertigo. He slumped forward over the neck of the horse and put his arms around the animal's neck to prevent himself from sliding out of the saddle.

'What's wrong, Travis?' Hester cried. 'Are you all right?'

Jordan stopped the horse and slithered to the ground. His senses were whirling, and for a few tense moments he could not find his equilibrium. There was a disconcerting buzzing sound in his ears and he closed his eyes. He shook his head and then opened his eyes to find the ground undulating. Nausea assailed him and he closed his eyes again. His hands were trembling violently. He sensed that his consciousness was fading, and exerted his will to fight the encroaching weakness. He could not afford to rest.

Hester's hand shook his right shoulder and Jordan risked a glance at his sister. Her worried face swam before his eyes and he clenched his teeth. He forced himself into a sitting position and lowered his face into his hands. The buzzing sound faded slowly from his ears and he looked up, thankful that the disconcerting bout of dizziness was receding.

'I must have banged my head when my horse went down,' he said, pushing himself to his feet.

Hester grasped him and held him

steady as he swayed. He shook off her hands and moved unsteadily to the waiting horse.

'You were unconscious when Hillyard brought you into Box J,' Hester said. 'You're suffering concussion, Travis.'

'I'll rest up after I've killed Farron.' He spoke through his teeth, and stepped up into the saddle and went on, fighting against the weakness that spilled up inside him.

Jordan's head was aching and he had trouble focusing his gaze on his surroundings. He pushed the horse into a faster gait and almost pitched out of the saddle. Hester stayed with him, calling words of encouragement as they continued towards Oak Bend. Jordan hardly heard her voice. He was having great difficulty staying upright in the jolting saddle.

A bullet crackled by Jordan's head and he reined in sharply, leaning to his right and diving for the ground as an echoing report came from behind. He snatched at his Winchester as he left the saddle but missed, and grunted as he hit the ground again. He rolled, and dizziness assailed him, but he finished up on his stomach peering along his back trail, and his pistol was in his hand although he had no recollection of drawing the weapon.

The rifle fired again and a slug hit the ground only inches in front of Jordan before whining away over his head. He blinked rapidly and his eyes slid into focus. A rider was coming towards him and he heaved a sigh when he recognized Braska, approaching with deadly intent. Hester suddenly appeared beside Jordan's horse, dragged a rifle from its saddle boot, and hurled the long gun in Jordan's direction. It hit the ground beside him and Jordan snatched it up.

'Get into cover, Hester,' he yelled, and worked the mechanism of the Winchester. A 44.40 cartridge clicked metallically into the breech.

Jordan blinked rapidly to clear his sight, thankful that his attack of giddiness seemed to have passed. He squinted through the sights of the rifle and drew a bead on the approaching Braska. The wounded gunman was having difficulty reloading his weapon. He was two hundred yards away and coming in at a gallop. Jordan waited until the gunman was levelling his weapon before squeezing his trigger. The flat crack of the Winchester flung a string of echoes across the range.

Braska dropped his gun and fell over backwards out of his saddle. Jordan shook his head and pushed himself to his feet. He staggered towards the horse and, as he made a great effort to regain the saddle, Hester called out to him.

'Travis, there's a bunch of riders. They've seen us and are turning this way.'

Jordan settled himself in the saddle and snatched up the reins before attempting to look at the newcomers. He cradled the Winchester in his left arm, which was paining him acutely. His head was aching and he had trouble spotting the approaching riders, but picked them out and recognized Two-Finger Dack leading them, followed by five tough-looking gunmen.

'Ride to town and alert Henry Forder,' Jordan rapped. 'Tell him to guard Dad. I'll tackle Dack and this bunch. Get moving, Hester, and ride for your life.'

He heard the clatter of hoofs as Hester obeyed, but his attention was on the riders coming at a gallop across the range. He looked around for cover, aware that he had to stop this bunch in its tracks, conscious now that he should have taken Dack when he had the chance. The riders came on, and the next instant they were shooting at Jordan and the range reverberated to the rapid sounds of deadly gunfire.

10

Jordan opened fire, and winced as the crash of the rifle flailed the silence, for the reports of the shooting sounded much louder than usual, jabbing at his eardrums like knife-thrusts. He clenched his teeth, sent a stream of slugs at Dack and his men, and was gratified to see one man fall out of his saddle. The rest swung away and rode in different directions as Jordan continued to shoot at them. Another man went down, and then the survivors were in cover and bullets came snarling into Jordan's position.

Jordan had no intention of fighting a set battle against Dack. He was worried about his father, and wanted to get at Farron before the crooked rancher could carry out his threat to kill Saul. He slid back out of cover, ran unsteadily to the waiting horse, and sprang into the saddle. Bullets crackled around him as he set out to cover the last miles to Oak Bend.

Dack and his men came out of cover and followed Jordan, but remained out of gunshot range. Jordan was satisfied that he was between Dack and the town. When he reached good cover on a ridge he reined in with only his head and shoulders showing above the skyline and fired at the pursuing riders as soon as they drew within range. One man dropped out of his saddle and the rest wheeled and rode back out of range. Jordan continued, his head aching from the shooting.

The last miles to town were passed in similar manner — riding and shooting — and, by the time Oak Bend appeared in the distance, Dack had only two men with him, and they would not come within rifle range of Jordan despite Dack's insistence. Jordan reined in one last time and waited for Dack to appear on his back trail, but the Flying D rancher had no further wish to flirt with certain death and rode off in a wide circle to reach town without confronting Jordan.

Impatience vibrated through Jordan. Farron would make for Doc Merrill's house the instant he reached Oak Bend, and Saul Jordan was practically defenceless. Jordan knew Hester would make a stand for their father, but the girl could not be expected to fight experienced gunmen. He swung his horse and rode fast for the distant town.

Jordan noted there were saddle-horses standing in the wide street, and a group of men had gathered in front of the law office. He galloped into the street, pistol in his right hand. He saw Hester talking to Henry Forder on the sidewalk but did not stop. He rode along to the doctor's house, and dismounted before his horse pulled up in a slither of dust. He staggered and almost dropped to his knees. His senses swirled and he paused, making an effort to summon up strength and willpower. His ears were buzzing again and his sight was troubled.

Voices were yelling from along the street and he turned and looked back at the law office. Hester was running towards him, waving. Jordan turned to the door of the doctor's house, knocked on it with the muzzle of his pistol, and waited impatiently for a reply.

He was still waiting when Hester reached him. She grasped his arm and pulled him around to face her.

'Dad's not here and Doc Merrill is in the law office for safety,' she said. 'Lance took Dad out of town about two hours ago. Forder tried to dissuade Lance but he wouldn't listen to reason.'

'Where did they go?' Jordan demanded.

'Lance hired a buggy and headed south with Dad. He knew it wasn't safe to return to Box J, and took Tom Sheldon, the stableman's son, along with him. If he hadn't taken Dad, Farron would have found him here.'

'South!' Jordan gazed along the street. 'Where would he go in that direction? Why did Doc let him take Dad?'

'Lance threatened Doc with a gun.'

'Did Farron ride in here?' Jordan was thankful the buzzing sound in his ears was abating.

'He did, and drew a gun on Forder, who told him Dad was no longer here. He rode out with one man, heading south. We'll have a job to catch up with him before he reaches that buggy, Travis.'

Jordan stifled a groan. 'I told Lance to sit tight in his hotel room. He's probably played right into Farron's hands. Go back to the law office, Hester, and stay there until I get back. Dack and some of his men are coming into town, and I want to find you still in one piece when I return.'

'Ride fast, Travis. You've got to catch up with Farron.'

Jordan climbed into his saddle and set off along the street. The sidewalks were deserted. He thundered past the hotel, heading out of town, and was nearing the stable when two riders emerged from the tall building and came towards him at a canter, sunlight glinting on the guns they were holding. He recognized one of them as Two-Finger Dack and pulled his horse down to a walk.

Jordan threw a glance over his shoulder back along the street and saw a rider approaching from that direction. Dack had him surrounded. He drew and cocked his gun and spurred his horse forward, aware that he had no time to waste here in town.

Dack opened fire, chasing out the brooding silence with the racket of rapid gunshots. A gun blasted in Jordan's rear and a slug cracked perilously close to him. He fired two shots at Dack and hauled on his reins as an alley opened up on his left. He caught a fleeting glimpse of Dack's horse going down, and bullets smacked into the woodwork at the corner of the alley as he sped into cover. He rode recklessly along the alley to the back lots, swerved the horse to the right, and headed south at a gallop, his ears ringing to the harsh echoes of the shooting.

With the town behind him, Jordan swung right to the trail and hammered over the hard ground. He could see the fresh wheel tracks of a buggy and pushed the horse into its top speed, but sensed that he would be too late to stop Farron, for the crooked rancher had more than a head start on him.

The range south of town was undulating and rough and the trail snaked left and right around huge rocks and tall-standing brush. Jordan topped a rise in the trail and peered ahead, his eyes narrowed. Sweat beaded his forehead. He felt ill, but pushed on relentlessly, and finally caught a glimpse of the buggy far ahead, shimmering in the heat haze. Fear stabbed through him when he realized it was motionless. The vehicle looked empty, and there were no signs of life around it.

Galloping on, the scene disappeared

abruptly as Jordan hit a down slope, and he wondered about Farron as he continued. The crooked rancher should be somewhere between him and the buggy.

He slowed as he approached the motionless vehicle, gun in hand, and checked his surroundings for Farron as he closed in. There was no sign of the rustler boss, and Jordan's heart lurched when he saw an inert figure lying on the seat of the buggy. He swung out of his saddle and hurried to the side of the vehicle.

The dead youth was a stranger to Jordan, and he had been expecting to see Lance. He paused with his gun poised while he looked around for tracks in the dust. He could see where two horses had stood, and guessed Farron had caught up with the buggy, which would account for the stable-man's son lying dead. But there was no sign of boot prints anywhere, and Jordan peered around, wondering what had become of his father and brother.

The silence was nerve-racking, the heat of the blazing sun almost too intolerable to bear.

A rifle cracked from behind and Jordan's horse fell with thrashing legs. Jordan jumped behind the buggy and peered back along the trail. He saw two riders a hundred yards away, and recognized Farron's diminutive figure. More shots crackled and he ducked, waiting for the storm to cease. When silence came he stood up to see the riders galloping back towards Oak Bend.

Jordan sagged and leaned against the buggy. Farron must have heard his fast approach and taken cover until he had passed. Jordan straightened and took stock of the situation. His horse was dead on the trail, he was several miles from Oak Bend, and Farron was on his way back there to continue his deadly search.

He took the horse from the buggy and saddled it with the gear from his dead mount. The harness-horse was not accustomed to a saddle and cavorted when he mounted it, but he brought it quickly under control and set off back to town, wondering what Lance had done. Had he remained in town with Saul, or had he left the buggy at some point between town and where Farron had caught up with it? But whatever his brother had done, Lance had kept their father out of Farron's hands, and Jordan was relieved that the crooked rancher had so far been thwarted.

Farron was well mounted and soon put distance between himself and Jordan. The town appeared on the horizon ahead and Jordan spurred his horse but failed to increase its pace. He saw Farron disappear into the main street and drew his pistol, hoping against hope to catch up with him before the crooked rancher could locate Lance and Saul.

Reaching the stable, Jordan hunkered down in his saddle when a gun blasted at him from the big open doorway of the barn. He had no time to waste and urged the horse forward, shooting into the gun smoke flaring around the edge of the door. His slugs bored through the woodwork, and a man staggered forward from its cover and pitched lifelessly to the ground.

Jordan whirled the horse and went on along the street. He saw Farron's horse standing in front of the hotel, and Two-Finger Dack was standing in the doorway of the building with one of his men. They started shooting as soon as Jordan drew within range, and a third gun opened up at Jordan from across the street opposite the hotel.

Gun racket shattered the silence hanging over Oak Bend. Jordan slid out of the saddle, gun flaming. He used the horse as a shield, facing the hotel and shooting across the animal's back, holding the reins in his left hand while the horse pranced and tried to bolt. Dack dropped to one knee but kept working his pistol, and Jordan heard a sickening thud as a bullet ploughed into the horse.

Jordan drew a bead on Dack and squeezed his trigger. Dack spun around and fell on his face on the sun-warped boards, but kept shooting and hit the horse again. Jordan ran for the cover of an alley mouth as the horse went crashing into the dust. The man opposite the hotel splintered woodwork around Jordan as he moved, and Jordan returned fire, teeth clenched and eyes narrowed. The man suddenly flung down his gun and took a jerky pace forward before falling on his face in the dust.

One gunman stood in front of the saloon still shooting at Jordan, who moved out into the open and went forward despite the lead coming at him. He drew a bead on the man's belt buckle and squeezed off a shot. The man fell back in the doorway of the hotel and dropped to the floor with only his feet protruding on to the sidewalk.

Echoes faded as Jordan continued. He staggered, assailed once again by a disconcerting unsteadiness that affected his head and eyes. His gun hand fell weakly to his side and he paused and leaned against the wall of a building, lowering his head as he fought to maintain his stability. His ears buzzed and nausea assailed him. He plucked fresh shells from his cartridge belt, broke his gun, and reloaded spent chambers. By the time the pistol was ready for further use the bad moment had passed, and Jordan went on.

Hester was coming along the sidewalk with a pistol in her hand. She was shouting at Jordan but he could not make out what she was saying. He paused at the doorway of the hotel and waited for her to reach him. As she drew nearer she repeated her words, and this time he got the message.

'Farron went into the hotel but Dad and Lance are not in there. I checked when you left town, and then asked around, but no one has seen them since they left in the buggy. Did you find the buggy, Travis?'

Jordan explained the events as he looked around to check out their surroundings.

'So what's happened to them?' Hester demanded. 'Where can they have gone?'

'At least Farron hasn't found them yet,' Jordan replied. 'Go back to the law office while I look for him. This town will not be safe until I've killed him.'

'You've shot your way right through Farron's crooked business,' Hester observed bitterly, 'and yet Farron himself is still alive.'

'He's about come to the end of his rope,' Jordan replied. 'All I want is a glimpse of him. I know he won't surrender to the law, so I've got to put him down in the dust.' He paused before asking, 'Why hasn't Forder taken a hand in this clean-up? He was all for law and order when I left town yesterday.'

'His two deputies were shot when Farron first arrived. Forder was scared Farron would release the prisoners in the cells so he stayed put in the jail.'

Jordan nodded. 'Let me get on. Get under cover, Hester. Farron went into the hotel and I've got to flush him out.'

Hester went back along the street and Jordan straightened. He was feeling better again, and checked his gun. There was throbbing pain in his left arm and shoulder but he ignored the discomfort and entered the hotel. Two men were standing in the lobby by the reception desk, and they raised their hands at his entrance. Neither appeared to be armed and Jordan confronted them.

'Abel Farron came in here a couple of minutes ago,' Jordan rasped. 'Where is he?'

'He went up the stairs, looking for someone. He didn't say who,' one of the men said.

'And he hasn't come down,' the other said. 'The shooting outside must have spooked him.'

'Is there a back door out of here?' Jordan asked.

'Sure. And back stairs leading to it.'

Jordan gritted his teeth. Farron was far from trapped, and his job would not be over until he had killed the crooked rancher. He wondered where his father and Lance were. They had left town in the buggy, but obviously left it before Farron caught up with it. He thought about it, and then went out to the sidewalk, stepped over Dack's body and walked to the street. He looked for wheel tracks in the dust and saw where the buggy had pulled in from the stable to pick up his father and brother and then wheeled around and headed back along the street, heading out of town, and Jordan followed them, gun in hand.

The wheel tracks passed town limits and Jordan stood gazing along the trail. Twenty yards on, the trail bent around a small stand of trees, and Jordan went to them, his eyes intent upon the ground. The buggy had stopped as soon as it was out of sight of the town and he saw two sets of boot-prints where someone had alighted. The boot-tracks went into the trees and then out to the right before heading for the livery stable twenty yards away.

Jordan started running towards the barn. Lance had played it smart. He had taken Tom Shelton with him to drive the buggy while he and Saul alighted and sought cover in the barn. The ploy had been successful, but Farron could have worked it out by now. Jordan reached the barn and ran inside.

He paused in the dim interior and looked around, listening intently for sound. He heard nothing but the stamp of a horse's hoof. Deadly silence enveloped the wooden building. His attention was drawn to the hay loft.

'Lance,' he called. 'This is Travis. Are you in here?'

There was no reply and he realized that he was holding his breath. He exhaled in a long sigh and leaned against a post as his senses flickered. His pistol felt almost too heavy to hold. He cuffed sweat from his forehead. A board creaked somewhere in the barn, alerting him, and he swung around, gun lifting. He caught the outline of a figure just inside the back door and dropped to his knees as a gun blasted, filling the barn with racket while a bullet crackled past his ear.

Jordan fired two shots, blinking against the flaring gun smoke, and when the smoke drifted the figure was gone. He did not know if he had scored a hit or not, and was torn between the need to find Saul and Lance and the desire to pursue his enemies.

A volley of shots hammered from along the street and Jordan pushed himself upright and went out to the front yard. Echoes were fading by the time he could look along the street into the town. Five saddle-horses were in front of the law office, moving swiftly as they hunted cover. One of the horses was galloping away in the opposite direction, and an inert figure lay stretched out in the dust. Jordan went towards the trouble spot, struggling against another bout of encroaching weakness. The four riders were across the street now, dismounting and turning to shoot into the law office. Jordan guessed they were more of Farron's men, but he had no idea where they had come from.

Jordan lifted his gun to continue the fight, but before he could start shooting a bullet smacked into the dust beside his right foot and he caught a flicker of movement from the roof of the saloon. He tossed a slug at a man silhouetted against the sky and ran for cover on the opposite side of the street, turning in the doorway of a dress shop and cocking his pistol. The man on the roof of the saloon had ducked out of sight, and as Jordan turned his gun on the men shooting into the law office, he became aware of the shop door being opened at his back.

Whirling, Jordan saw a man emerging from the shop. His right index finger tensed around the curved metal of his trigger, and then he flipped his gun sideways, for he was looking at his brother Lance.

'Travis, Dad is in here with me,' Lance said. He was holding a pistol. His face was tense, filled with concern. 'We've been hiding out. I've prayed for you to get back to town. Do you know Farron is here on the loose?'

'I know, but I haven't set eyes on him yet. How is Dad? You sure had me worried when I heard you'd pulled out in a buggy. But I think you prevented Farron from getting to Dad. Stay put here while I finish off this business. Keep your gun handy. There's no telling where Farron is right now.'

'Dad is OK, and don't worry, I'll guard him.' Lance spoke fiercely.

Jordan turned away. Shots were still hammering along the street. He peered in the direction of the law office and saw three men firing into the front of the office. A single gun was replying. He checked his pistol and moved on, determined to put an end to the violence. His first shot at the trio brought one of them around and slugs came at him. He steadied himself, lifted his gun, and rejoined the fight, walking towards the law office.

He started shooting, and the man opposing him fell away. The two remaining gunnies looked round, and then started withdrawing. Jordan was in no mood to quit and cut loose at them. One went down immediately. The other turned to flee, and was only two paces from an alley mouth when a slug caught him and sent him tumbling into the dust.

Echoes began to fade and an uneasy silence settled over the street. No one moved anywhere. Jordan walked along the street, gun poised in his right hand, aware that it was not over yet. Farron was skulking somewhere, like a timber wolf awaiting a final chance to seize its prey.

The door of the law office was opened and Henry Forder emerged, carrying a pistol in his left hand. Blood was showing on his right shoulder.

'Hey, Travis,' he called. 'Have you nailed Farron?'

'Not yet. I haven't seen him.'

'He went into the bank. I spotted him. He had Hester with him.'

Jordan turned cold inside. He turned instantly and went towards the bank, cursing himself for not thinking of it before. Farron would need funds to make a run for it. He reached the sidewalk in front of the bank, and at that moment glass tinkled and he saw Farron at the window, a gun in his hand coming into line to open fire. Farron was hard-faced, desperate.

'I got your sister in here, Jordan,' he called. 'If you wanta save her life you better get out of here until I've moved out.'

Jordan wondered at Farron's mentality. There was no sign of Hester, and the crooked Rafter F rancher was in full view. He lifted his pistol and fired in one swift movement. Farron jerked and spun away from the shattered window. Jordan ran across the sidewalk and hurled himself at the door of the bank, his impetus carrying him in over the threshold. He lost his balance and sprawled on the floor, twisting to cover Farron, who was lying on the floor, his gun discarded.

Hester came forward from behind the banker's desk, her face pale. She paused to kick Farron's gun away, and then bent to examine Farron. Jordan lowered his gun, aware that Farron was dead. It was beginning to dawn on him that it was all over. He had shot the hell out of his family's trouble. His ears were ringing from the shooting, but now the echoes had faded away and he pushed himself to his feet.

He slid an arm around Hester's shoulder and they left the bank and walked towards the dress shop. Townsfolk were emerging from the buildings. The sun was way over in the west and heading for the horizon. Jordan took a long breath of clean air to rid his lungs of gun smoke. It was a nice evening now the shooting was over, and the future looked rosy to Jordan.